SANDS AND STARLIGHT

A WONDER TALE

CHARLOTTE E. ENGLISH

PART ONE: BARADIR

1

Twilight, and a hush cloaked the darkening sands. To a stranger, the silence might be oppressive, born as it was of the vast emptiness of the steppe. To Baradir, the silence was expectant.

He paused in the lee of a rocky promontory, sheltered from the dry winds that swept past in a haze of dust and sand. One precious skin of water went to refresh the three camels of his caravan; they drank greedily, thick lips slurping noisily. Baradir, dreaming of mint-laced tea in a clear glass, satisfied himself with a swallow or two. *Soon,* he promised himself. He need only wait while the sun sank beyond the horizon, taking the vestiges of the burning day away with it.

Thirst and hunger lengthened the minutes; twilight glimmered on in a haze of low light. Baradir found a large rock, still glowing with the day's heat, and seated himself cross-legged atop its storm-smoothed surface. Five days' travel overland from Zahele had brought him to this remote spot; a familiar enough journey, though one he had not made in some years. For the first few days, he had met other traders along the road; once, he had successfully bartered two of the gold-threaded silks he'd procured in Parsas for a quantity of frankincense, and a ceramic jar filled to the brim with cinnamon. The trade pleased him, particularly since he had also gained a third article: a glass bottle, too plain to fetch a high price. Its former owner had been eager to be rid of it.

To Baradir, the thing was no mere trinket. Blue glass, ethereally translucent beneath its coating of grime; a simple shape, almost unornamented, but its neck tightly stoppered, and sealed with copper. Its scant heft might herald the bottle's lack of contents, but it lied. Baradir withdrew the bottle from a pocket in his cloak. For a moment he simply sat and held it, silently appreciative of his good fortune. Gently, he smoothed dirt away with his thumb.

An eerie glimmer of light sparked to life somewhere within.

The sweet, haunting notes of harp-song drifted along the breeze, a chang in full flow, and he looked up sharply. Heat shimmered fiercely before him, the horizon rippling like clear water. The scents of oranges and rosewater and cardamom teased at his nose, and — yes — fresh mint.

Dust whirled up, swift and hot, making Baradir cough. When it cleared, the Starlight Bazaar was open, a burst of bright colour blossoming in the midst of the parched sands.

Baradir rose to his feet, tucking his precious acquisition back into his pocket, and descended towards the night market, stumbling in his haste to reach it. Hanee, Fasee and Talee broke into an eager lope behind him, kicking up dust and sand with their leathery toes. Beyond the gilded gates, orange groves were in full flourish; thence came the heady aromas of citrus and orange-blossom. White petals carpeted the ground.

The souk formed the centre of the Bazaar: three rings of bright tents, sprawling in brazen offer of plenty over the pallid sand. Traders' voices split the cooling night air, offering enchanted silks and heady rose wine; ethereal moon-pearls and night-lustre gems; eternal frangipani and phoenix feathers; and, of more immediate interest to Baradir, hot, fresh bread, crisp and thin; orange-blossom cream custards; and, best of all, syrup of mint stirred through water cold as snow. He paused at each of these vendors, turning his eyes away from their neighbours proffering trinkets, enchantments and treasures. Later. Soon.

Baradir sat beneath an orange tree as he ate, and watched the lights dancing in its branches. Talee fastened her thick lips into the fabric of his cloak and tugged, receiving for her reward a handful of dates from his pocket. A young woman approached, put a cup of rose wine into his hands, and retreated, her eyes laughing above the gauzy mist of her veil. Baradir took a breath, and a sip, and sat back, his heart eased.

He watched the bustle of the Bazaar whirl past for almost an hour before the jewels trader found him.

'How slow you are,' he said as Iskandar approached. The trader, resplendent in wine-red embroidered sirwal, wore a silken turban wound around his head. 'Is two years avoidance not long enough?' Baradir added.

'Avoidance?' answered Iskandar, and looked down upon Baradir with raised brows. Red jewels glinted in his thick black beard. Seen with Baradir's left eye, the jewels roiled with sorcerous potency. 'I could not have caught up with you before now; not if I had tried,' said Iskandar. 'And, for your interest, I did.'

'I have travelled far,' admitted Baradir.

Iskandar snorted. 'I hear of you in Zahele, I hear of you in Parsas. I hear of you up and down the Horns of Jubarut. You are spotted somewhere along the Ahvadannar, washed away, imagined dead; but then! Next, you are sighted at Al-Kabes, at Sulanah.' An engraved copper samavar floated in Iskandar's wake upon a tray of wrought brass, attended by a pair of gilded cups. Iskandar set about pouring tea as he spoke, and from somewhere produced a cake thick with pistachios and almonds, which he put into Baradir's hands. 'The only places I hear nothing of you are the Bazaars, and I wonder: why should Baradir bin Samar cease to attend the starlit streets? If one of us has been avoiding the other, old friend, it was not I.'

Weeks of living off little but dates and water made Baradir more than happy to accept these comforts, despite the quantity of bread he had but lately consumed. He sipped tea, tasting honey and rose, and considered his reply.

'Have you found it?' was not what he had planned to say.

'Tsk. You think I would be wasting your time and mine with comestibles, had I such news for you? This news I would already have given you.'

It was the response Baradir had expected, but still his heart sank. Pistachios crunched between his teeth as he thought.

'Your wanderings have brought no word either, I am to take it?' said Iskandar.

Baradir shook his head. 'Twice I imagined myself close, but... no. There are tales, of course, of glimpses caught here or there, but.' He sighed. 'I cannot discover that there is any more to these stories than a fleeting mirage, or a fevered imagination.'

Iskandar sat back, hands wrapped around his own fragrant cup, and looked long at Baradir. 'How bad is it now?'

The words would not come. Instead, Baradir passed a hand over his face. Coloured glass glinted in the soft-lit darkness.

Iskandar stared, though he was not so appalled as Baradir had feared. 'That eye,' he said, pointing a thick finger at the left side of Baradir's face. 'Can you see out of it?'

'In a manner of speaking.' He let his true visage show for a moment longer, giving Iskandar a clear view of the enchanted glass that had, so insidiously, crept from his heart to claim a finger and a thumb; some part of his throat; his left cheek; and, at last, one eye. It was not wholly true that he could see nothing out of that eye. He could see nothing ordinary, that was the truth, and that was all Iskandar need know.

'What happens when it has taken all of you?' said Iskandar — refusing, as ever, to shy from harsh thoughts, brutal truths.

'I do not know,' said Baradir, and passed his glass-touched hand back over his face. His mottled visage faded, replaced once more by the uninterrupted dark brown skin, the black beard and black eyes that had once been his own. 'I shall become an arcane thing, of a kind never before seen.' A whisper of sound caught his attention, coming somewhere from his right. He did not turn his head, nor give any outward sign that he had heard, but every sense strained, alert. Was someone there?

No. A bird, or a sand cat only. He relaxed.

Iskandar ate a few cakes, until syrup gleamed stickily in his beard. 'Well, then,' he said, licking his fingers clean. 'If it is not the looked-for news which brings you to the Bazaar tonight, what has prompted the visit?'

Baradir drew forth the simple glass bottle, but pulled it back when Iskandar tried to touch it. 'Do not get it any dirtier, I pray you.'

'It has some hidden property, I suppose.' Iskandar wiped his fingers on an ivory silk handkerchief.

Baradir touched his two glass fingers to the bottle, and light shone once more at its core. 'I believe it to contain an enchantment of some sort—'

'A jinn?' laughed Iskandar. 'And you found this, where, in some junk room? They are not so easily contained, my friend, for all that the stories say otherwise.'

'Not a jinn.'

'Have you opened it?'

'Of course not.'

Iskandar shrugged, and sat back. 'You will fetch a fine price for it here, no doubt.'

'I don't seek to sell. Not yet. I want information.'

'Is it my counsel you seek?'

'Among others.'

'And why mine? Little spirits, they are not my area of expertise.'

'Because of this.' Baradir turned the bottle, until its stopper pointed Iskandar's way. When he traced his glass-etched thumb over the copper seal, a jewel lit up, flaring with sudden fire.

Iskandar's eyes widened. 'Oh. That's quite another thing.' He took the bottle, and this time Baradir let him. In the jewel-sorcerer's hands, the gem shone almost as brightly. It was a deep blue moon-pearl, deeply inset, inert until brought blazing to life. 'Well,' he said, turning the bottle about in his hands. 'I will buy it for that alone, and I'll give you a good price.'

'I'll remember the offer.' Baradir held out his hand for his treasure.

Iskandar's grin flashed white. 'Fortune favours you, you dog.' He returned the bottle, with a show of nonchalance which did not for an instant fool Baradir.

His words left Baradir unmoved, for he knew, so much to his cost, that they were untrue. And why should Lady Fortune favour him, anyway? What had he ever done to deserve the distinction? Fate and Fortune: they did not work at random. Late they may be, slow they may be, but in time, a man got what he had earned.

Watching a duskwing moth settle upon a nearby desert rose bush, its delicate legs clinging to the blushing pink blossom, Baradir thought he saw something else: the flash of bright eyes, there and then gone again.

He straightened. 'Night is ever short,' he said. 'I had better make my enquiries while there's some of it left.'

Iskandar laughed up at him as Baradir rose to his feet. 'Short? You have hours and hours, my friend.'

'And it's a big bazaar.' Baradir bowed formally. 'I shall find you again before dawn. We'll drink a glass of something.'

'Wine,' said Iskandar, getting to his feet also. 'What else is there?'

Baradir walked the Bazaar alone after that, pausing occasionally to exchange a bow and a few words with some acquaintance or another, but declining all further invitations to draw up a cushion and accept a cup of wine. He began at the outer edges of the market and worked his way in, passing by (with some regret) those vendors selling tea and fragrant stew and fried dough, and those offering ethereal silks or pungent incense or charms; his attention was all for the jewel traders, like Iskandar, or those selling what had once been his own specialty: ensorcelled glass.

He did not meet with much success. Everywhere he showed the bottle, eyes lit up with interest, and avarice; fingers stroked the bottle's smooth surface with covetous delight, and offers were made. But information proved harder to come by than currency, for no one could or would explain the nature of the trinket. Perhaps they could not. They saw a fine, rare jewel and traces of sorcery; at this market, that was enough.

More than one pressed him to name the bottle's source, but that he would not do.

Arrived at last at the heart of the Bazaar, and with little to show for his labours, Baradir stood alone and in thought, uncertain of his next course of action. Of all places, the Starlight Bazaar had seemed the one place guaranteed to furnish him with the answers he sought; if it could not, where else could he go? He must travel on to the next night market, and the next, and the next. His heart sank at the prospect, for his feet were weary of walking, his mouth weary of sand upon his tongue and dust coating his throat. He wanted, needed, rest.

Rest, he thought, in searing self-mockery. *When did you begin to believe that you deserved peace, sorcerer?*

Hanee and Talee had wandered off; they would be found later, wandering the outskirts of the Bazaar, chewing with dreamy contentment upon some hapless, succulent plant. Fasee, though, trailed behind Baradir like a faithful dog, too young yet for the self-possession and independence of her sisters in service. Though she frequently bumped him with her nose, lumbered sideways into his path, and on one memorable occasion trod heavily upon his foot, he was secretly grateful for the company. The simplicity of animals had ever been a comfort. Surreptitiously, he palmed another handful of dates and fed them to her, stroking her bristly nose.

The crowd whirled around them both, adapting with remarkable serenity to the presence of a fully-grown camel with her unlovely feet planted squarely upon the mosaic tableau that marked the centre. Only one person caught his eye: a young woman, gauzily veiled, her figure draped in loose silks the colour of desert roses. A smile lingered in those eyes, and he remembered her. The laughing generosity with which she had presented him with wine — and not stayed to claim a reward.

Half-unknowing, he followed in her wake.

She saw him, and knew herself pursued, for several times she glanced back. Every flash of those velvet-black eyes drew him farther onward, though he hardly knew what he was about. Even the pressure of Fasee's teeth upon his elbow had little power to slow his advance.

Nothing could; not until he had retraced his steps back to the outskirts of the Bazaar, weaving his way through traders in turbans and kaftans, through buyers in veils and jewels. A thousand scents assaulted his nostrils, colours dazzled his eyes, and still he went on, and on—

—until brought to an abrupt halt, his face in the dirt, the wind knocked out of him. He had fallen over something he had not, in his haste, observed to be in his path.

Dazed and confused, he looked up — and straight into the eyes of the woman blocking the way between him and his fair tormentor. Not so finely dressed, this lady, though hints of a rich perfume rolled off her. She wore a midnight-blue scarf over her hair, but no veil; her sirwal and curled shoes were of a cloth to match, lightly embroidered in silver. A cloak of deep green hid her figure. Lines around her eyes, and the corners of her mouth, spoke of years lived and laughter, though there was no trace of mirth about her now. Hands on hips, she surveyed Baradir as he lay there in the dirt, and her black eyes were hard as onyx.

'Baradir,' she said, and it was a velvet voice, roughened with sand. 'Is that whom I have the honour of addressing?'

'That is my name,' he allowed, and cautiously sat up. Something about the woman's iron demeanour left him unsure of his safety, if he attempted to stand.

'Baradir bin Samar,' she said.

He inclined his head.

'But you have an older name, do you not?'

Baradir went still and watchful. 'I have always been known as Baradir, lady,' he said quietly.

'I dare say, and by another hundred names besides. You are a sorcerer.'

Baradir's eyes narrowed. He recalled where he had seen those eyes before. 'You have been following me about the Bazaar, lady, and I doubt not that the sorcerous damsel of the rosy silks was your doing, also.'

'An illusion only,' said the woman, and looked upon him with contempt. 'How easily may a man be led by the nose.'

Tired of grovelling before so much disdain, Baradir drew himself slowly to his feet. 'What can you mean by setting upon me in this fashion? Pray state your business, the sooner that I may depart upon my own.'

'You are Ibn Samar.'

'I do not know of whom you speak.'

The woman advanced upon him by a step. 'You know full well of whom I speak. The greatest sorcerer of his age, none to touch him for power—'

'Lady, pray consider—'

'—and that power ate away at his heart and soul and turned both to ash, and not the greatest of afreets could equal this sorcerer after, not for misdeeds and crimes—'

'Lady, I beg you—' Baradir held up his hands, but she was unstoppable.

'But he was punished at last, for his own heart turned to cold glass in his chest, and they say that this glass spread, and ever shall, until it has devoured every inch of him, and then—'

'*Lady.*' Baradir's voice cut across hers like the lash of a whip. 'What you speak of is impossible. Were I this man, I would have lived far beyond a mortal's span of years. Would I not?'

'Enough years for two men at least,' she said, with the faintest of smiles.

'Then I cannot be him, and you will excuse me.' Baradir made his bow, but the woman — damn her — caught his wrist in a grip of iron.

'I saw it on you,' she said.

Baradir thought of his momentary display for Iskandar's benefit, and sighed. 'It is not the behaviour of a woman of honour to spy upon her fellows.'

'I could not help it. The very earth announced your presence, the moment you set foot over the threshold of the Bazaar.'

And Baradir sighed again, for had he not avoided the Bazaar for just such a reason? 'Say that I am this sorcerer,' Baradir said, allowing a hint of iron to creep into his own voice. 'Did you accost me for the pleasure of insulting me? You cannot do a better job of that than I can do myself, lady. I assure you that you waste your time.'

'No,' she said, looking at him strangely. 'Undoubtedly you deserve such abuse, but — no. No, I would demand something of you.'

Baradir smiled inwardly at her manner of leaping straight over the word *ask*. 'What shall it be, then? Tell me quickly, for I tire.'

'A man of your age would.'

'A few insults, then. I am not to be spared entirely.'

The woman pressed her lips together, as though holding back another barrage of the same. To his surprise, he detected a flash of remorse in her hard black eyes — and even, perhaps, a hint of desperation. 'I am sorry,' she said.

Baradir bowed. This was not a woman to lightly offer an apology.

'I need your help,' she said.

'I had guessed as much, lady.'

'I am Yasmine.'

Baradir merely bowed, again, and waited.

'In a town a hundred parasangs from here,' she began, 'there was another sorcerer.'

'My felicitations.'

'He was once all my joy,' she said with quiet dignity, and Baradir regretted his sarcasm. 'But he is... gone. Vanished.'

'Why should you lay this problem before me, lady?' interrupted Baradir.

'Because the sorcerer I've named is my son.'

'That is not what I asked. Why do you lay this problem before *me*?'

'Because of the manner of his disappearance. One night, Ibn Samar, he came to me with a fantastic tale. Shall you hear it?'

'I had much rather not.'

'A tale of a palace.'

In spite of himself, Baradir went still, further protests dying away unspoken. 'A palace?' he echoed.

'A palace like no other, for this one was made — so my son swore — all of ensorcelled glass. Does that sound in any way familiar, sorcerer?'

Baradir could only swallow.

'This palace,' she continued, 'was grander and more beautiful than any palace had ever been before (so my son said), and so overflowing with enchantment that it possessed the ability —

among its many wonders — of vanishing with the dawn. Is that not remarkable?'

'Quite,' said Baradir, calmly again, for once the first shock of recognition had passed he had regained his composure.

'The day came, of course, when away went this precious palace, and my son with it, and neither has come back. What, then, must a mother do? Why, if she is clever she will seek the one who created the wonder in the first place. And there is but one palace out of legend that answers to my son's general description, Ibn Samar.'

'You fascinate me.'

'That palace is yours. If anyone can find what has become of it, it must be you.'

The woman rattled on, plans and entreaties mingling together in her cool recital, but Baradir's thoughts were turned elsewhere.

His palace. Could it truly be? Yes, of course it could. It must.

And again, yet again, he came to hear of it too late. The palace was long gone.

'Yasmine.' Baradir cut her off in the midst of yet another winding sentence. 'I am not who you imagine me to be, and I cannot help you.' The words were a lie, yet also a truth; for while Ibn Samar could have assisted the woman (whether he *would* or not being a different question), Baradir bin Samar was... powerless.

Nay, worse than powerless. Brimming with sorcery he could not in any safety use.

Crippled.

She looked long at him, in silence, and he had ample opportunity to enjoy the sadness and contempt in her eyes. Then, at last, she bowed, stiff and formal. 'Forgive me for imposing upon your time,' she said, and turned away.

Baradir watched her go. She walked with a straight spine, and unbowed head; a proud woman.

Fasee bit at his sleeve.

'Yes, yes,' he said, distractedly feeding her dates. Yasmine vanished into the crowd, leaving him alone in the dark and quiet beyond the circle of lights and laughter. 'We go on,' he informed Fasee — and Talee, who came up on his other side and lipped at his hair. 'All the way to the Wilds of Kemasar, good ladies, and the next Bazaar. You are with me still, no?'

They indicated their joint approval by the ready speed with which they devoured his offering of fruit.

'Good,' he murmured, staring still in the direction in which Yasmine had gone. 'For what would I be, without you?'

2

THE VAST EXPANSE OF the Silversands stood between Baradir and the wide, swift-flowing Ahvadannar, and the Kemasar Wilds beyond, for he had traversed but three days' worth of the bleak desert to reach the night market. Many days of privation and danger lay before him; too many to brave alone?

Early in the morning, when the fiery sun had not long since soared above the horizon, Baradir set the saddle upon Talee's back, draped her heavy blue blankets over, and mounted: the better to see, from such a height, and to save his feet from the pale, burning sand besides. But before he set his little caravan in motion, Fasee and Hanee falling into their accustomed places beside their strongest sister, he drew forth from inside his cloak a prize possession: a jewel.

It was not a thing that would have attracted much notice, or brought a great price, anywhere but at the night markets, for it was naught but a globe of crystal-clear quartz. Perfect it might be, in its shape and clarity, but only his left eye perceived the depths concealed within the sphere, or the drift of mist and air, like sleeping clouds, that stirred at its heart.

He held the trinket high, his strong, sun-darkened fingers clasped tightly around it.

At first, the jewel remained tranquil, and his hopes rose. But then a spark of lightning lit at its core, and cloudy wisps gathered and darkened and began to roil.

'A day at most,' he informed Talee, and put away the jewel. 'Time, then, to waken Iskandar's "little spirits".' He kept the bottle close at hand, like the jewel, and soon retrieved it. Had it somehow procured for itself a still deeper coat of grime, since last night? Truly, the glass wore dirt like strings of the finest jewels. Baradir polished it upon a fold of his dark cloak, and again caught that glimpse of pale light stirring to life within. Nothing like firelight, that sleepy glimmer, or the sun's fierce glow. No, it was the serene shimmer of moonlight on rainwater...

He carried the bottle to his mouth and put his lips to the glass. He spoke to it in a language no longer known, save to some sparse few sorcerers of the arcane, and with every slippery, coiling syllable that met the air, the light grew stronger.

The glass chilled beneath his fingers: the cool not of ice but of deep river waters. Dew blossomed on its surface, and ran down the sides.

And he felt himself drawn, clear and true, to the north-west.

'Thank you,' he told it, in the same ancient tongue, and set Talee's face to the north-west.

All the long day through, he kept the mysterious bottle in his left hand, and followed the course it set. And by nightfall, the distant branches of an oasis appeared on the featureless horizon: shade, and water, and safety.

His spirits rose at the sight, and Talee lifted her bristled nose to the wind, scenting lush vegetation upon the air. But something else caught her senses, too, for when he urged her to quicken her weary pace, she dug her toes into the sand and came to a halt.

'Talee, Talee, we are so close, do not give up now.' He stroked her neck, whispered soothing words, and waited with as much patience as he could muster. Her coarse fur was thick with sand and dirt, and his hand came away much begrimed, but this he ignored. 'Talee, just a little farther. Come now, onward.'

She would not move. And then came Fasee and Hanee, leaving their places in the line to flank their sister, and the three drew together into a wary, miserable knot.

Baradir's heart sank. He had seen this behaviour before, and it augured nothing good. As his camels dipped their heads low and huddled together, he sat straighter, chin lifted, eyes scanning the sky.

Nothing yet appeared of the disaster to come but a quickening of the wind, and a stirring of the sand beneath Talee's feet. Clouds roiled in the firmament, piled high; were the two related?

'How long?' he murmured. They might reach the oasis within half an hour, an hour at most, but that was not soon enough. He withdrew his clear jewel again, almost dropping it in his haste, and held it up. The glass flashed and churned, all turbulence; he put it away, and dismounted.

The wind blew from the east. Hastening as much as he could, coaxing his camels along with a mixture of comforting words and sharp pokes, he led his little party towards the beckoning oasis, praying for time enough. But the wind whipped the folds of his cloak around his body, and stole the scarf from his hair, and the sands began to dance.

He stopped, and fumbled through Hanee's load of bags for a treasure, almost impossible to discover among the layers of silks and cottons stored therein. Fool that he was, for he had arranged it thus deliberately; anyone looking for a small bundle of embroidered silk among his effects would never find it in time... and now nor could he.

Growing desperate, he unhooked the bag and turned it upside down over the sand, heedless of his precious fabrics tumbling to the ground. There — a flash of lapis-blue and sea-green and gold gilt thread. He snatched it up, unwound the ribbons that secured its precise folds, and held it carefully aloft. One of its scant remaining folds he undid, with deliberate care.

The silk leapt from his hands and sprang into life, spilling forth billows of silk brocade and linen and fine cotton. Reams of coloured fabric danced upon the spiralling winds, and then, draping themselves over nothing in particular, they became a tent, richly appointed and expansive. A split in the front opened itself wide and tied its two sides up, and a soft light shone from within, inviting Baradir inside.

Not an instant too soon, for the winds howled, now, around his ears, hurling sand and dust into his flinching face. He looked up, and wished he had not, for a wall of pale sand roared towards him, distant yet but closing far too fast. And, as he had feared, no ordinary sand storm was this, for the storm-clouds on the horizon had built higher and heavier, dark purple like an old bruise, and shot through with lightning.

Not a drop of rain fell. Instead, the air swirling about his ears shrieked and howled with unearthly voices, and his skin tingled and burned. The arcane winds of an unnatural storm. He stared, half mesmerised, dwarfed and vulnerable beneath the oncoming onslaught as the sky darkened.

Night swallowed the desert, all at once, and Fasee began to tremble.

'Move,' he ordered himself, and took a gulp of air. Moving with tremulous haste, he took up the lead-ropes of his three beloved camels and half dragged them through the split in the silks. With a faint whisper, the makeshift door closed itself up behind him, and left him alone with his beasts in a space of prismatic colour.

The tempest abated, the buffeting winds fading to nothing. Baradir's ears rang in the sudden silence. He cast a quick, uneasy glance up at the silken roof of his shelter, but it held. Of course it held. Nothing could assail his pavilion for long. That was one of the problems with the thing.

Its capricious nature was another. Baradir dared not draw aside the silks to see where, in all the kingdoms, he would emerge once he left the pavilion's shelter; not yet. He only knew that it would be anywhere but where he had gone in.

Fasee trembled still. He spoke to her and her sisters in gentle tones as he settled them in their customary corner. An oversized samavar, like Iskandar's but larger and less ornate, awaited a word from him to leap into life; he gave it, and presently poured out the weak tea favoured by his camels, and the stronger tea he preferred for himself. He soaked dried lemon and orange peel in the cooling waters before he imbibed the beverage, and laced the concoction with orange flower water. Seating himself cross-legged in the centre of the pavilion, he let his weary gaze wander the flimsy walls of his compact abode as he drank, his soul as much refreshed by the light and colour as was his body by the brew. The silks were vividly painted, like stained glass; images of far-off, beloved Sulanah surrounded him, a vision of the city as it had been in his youth. Every scene was drawn directly from his own memories, fixed there by enchantments that were, in these diminished days, beyond his power.

How many folds remained in the silk? A scant few. And yet, he must leave the familiar space, and soon. Always, he must leave.

But first, he could sleep — for once, in perfect safety.

Baradir wound himself in precious Xingqing blankets: cloud-light and cool, sun-velvet and warm, they were all things at need, and so priceless he dared not remove them from the pavilion. Once, and only once, had he stepped beyond his silken walls and found himself in that enchanted kingdom, a place any trader like himself would give an eye to behold.

These, too, he must someday lose.

Baradir lay alone, eyes open upon the florid walls of the only home he knew, until weariness swallowed him down into slumber.

❧ ☙

He woke with the importunate woman, Yasmine, in his thoughts. Curiously well-informed as to his history, she was; so desirous had he been of dispensing with her company, he had not given the fact much thought. Not only had she correctly guessed his identity, she had betrayed a more comprehensive knowledge of his life than he had imagined anyone could now possess, save himself. And how had she chanced to be in just the bazaar he had, at length, chosen to visit, and on the right night? On the watch for him, yes; she had said as much. But how had she known?

And what was she doing stalking the Starlight Bazaars, so far from home, in search of Ibn Samar?

Word of his travels was circulating. Iskandar had said as much. But Iskandar, at least, knew for whom to ask, and would recognise the small signs of his passage that would pass others by.

How had Yasmine tracked him so successfully?

How had she ever come to hear his name?

The matter cost him some disquiet, as he rose with great reluctance from the comfort of his makeshift bed. He wished, now, that he had not dismissed the woman so speedily, and that he had not run away from her. Alarm had done the mischief. He was not accustomed to finding himself welcome, not by those who knew what he was.

He would not see the woman again, in all likelihood. His refusal to be bent to her schemes had been too decided for further pursuit. Dismissing the matter, Baradir advanced upon the door of his pavilion, and carefully twitched the silk aside. Putting his good eye to the inch-wide gap, he took a long look beyond.

What struck him first was the aroma. The fragrances of a thousand flowers enveloped him, for before him lay a splendid garden. Low, verdant bushes with scented, gold-veined leaves were laid out in curving rows, housing great beds of sunset-hued desert roses and pale evening jasmine. He saw lilies dressed in blood-carmine hues, frilled acacia blossoms, and a host of blooms to which he could put no name. Winding streams ran this way and that, pearly green plants afloat here and there upon their clear, placid waters.

Overwhelmed by the medley of perfumes, Baradir sneezed.

Nothing about the garden gave him any hint as to where in all the kingdoms it was situated, but at least there was no sign of danger. And it was a vast improvement over the treacherous storm from which he had narrowly escaped.

'Once,' he said, as he roused his camels from slumber, 'I stepped out of that silken door and straight into a great battle. You will remember it, Talee, no? We were almost skewered alive a thousand times, by men too blood-frenzied to distinguish a traveller from a sabre-wielding soldier. We will take a garden over a war, however pungent.' The camels liked the perfumed space as little as he, and sneezed in triplicate as he chivvied them over the threshold. But they stood placidly enough, showing none of the distress they had felt at the onset of the storm.

Baradir uttered his least favourite word. Upon this signal, the enchanting pavilion collapsed in a puff of dust and mist, and swiftly restored itself to its innocent-seeming pose as a bundle of cloth. Baradir glumly regarded the scant remaining folds, and with a sigh, put the bundle away.

This done, he had leisure to look about himself more fully. Immediately his attention was caught by a grand fountain of black marble, rising majestically from the midst of those scented bushes. Water poured into the skies in great plumes, emanating from a dozen ornamented spouts, and fell in artful streams to the ground. The waters were not clear: they were the vivid azure of a desert sky at noon. Then, as he watched, their hue shifted to a serene jade colour, followed by the hazy purple of amethyst jewels.

Baradir drifted nearer.

'You must not drink from the fountain,' said a mild voice.

Startled, Baradir stopped, and looked about himself. He had seen no sign of another person in the gardens, nor heard chatter or footfall to indicate an occupying party — until now. But he saw no one.

'Why should I not?' he answered.

'You must not,' repeated the voice. 'Without first making an offering.'

'To whom am I to make this offering?'

'Why, to the fairy of the waters. Do you not know into whose garden you are come?'

Baradir had continued to approach the fountain throughout this exchange, though by slower steps. Still he saw no one. But, perched upon the branch of a strange, pale tree, arching some way over his head, was a large bird clad in plumage of malachite-green and indigo. Its beak and claws were silver, and its eyes copper-bright. Its head tilted under Baradir's scrutiny, and it clacked its gleaming silver beak. A long, long tail of glimmering feathers swept almost to the ground behind it.

'Is it you I address?' said Baradir.

Those coppery eyes simply stared into his, and the bird — if it was the bird who spoke — made no answer.

'Very well,' said Baradir. 'Tell me of this fairy, whose garden I have infiltrated without intent.'

'That cannot be, for no one comes here save with her leave.'

'Unless he comes by enchantments ancient and strange, as I have.'

The bird's head tilted. 'No enchantment can prevail here but that she wills it to be so.'

Baradir blinked. 'Well then, I must imagine myself welcome. Where is this fairy, that I might pay my respects?'

'Have you an offering prepared?'

'What manner of offering might please this being?'

'You might return my child to me,' said a new voice.

Baradir turned. Perched upon the fountain's edge, in a spot that had hitherto stood empty, was a woman perfectly strange to him. She had black hair like his own, though hers fell in waves to her waist. Her eyes, though, were the colour of ocean waters, and her skin the milk-white of sea pearls. She wore a gown of sea spray and river water; motes of ice and sea spray glittered in her hair, and hung about her throat.

'Lady,' he said, with the low bow of true respect, for he recognised a great power when he saw one.

The fairy of the waters made no acknowledgement of the gesture. Those eyes, serene as a placid lake and yet hard as ice, remained fixed coolly upon him, and he could read nothing of their expression. 'My child,' she repeated.

'Forgive me, lady, I know not of what you speak—' he said, but stopped, for he remembered. The glimmer of moonlight on water he'd seen stirring in the depths of his humble blue-glass bottle. And that lustrous moon-pearl at its neck. 'The little spirit. Lady, I swear to you I did not trap her there.'

'That may be so,' she allowed. 'Yet neither did you free her.'

'I—' He swallowed. 'Forgive me. I stood in sore need—'

'How so?'

'I needed her guidance to reach an oasis before—'

'And did you arrive at your oasis?' she interrupted.

'No, I— we were—' he stopped, and swallowed. The storm had been an unnatural force, that much he had swiftly discovered. Had it been no coincidence? Was it no coincidence, either, that his pavilion had delivered him here?

'Not so little a spirit,' he said, softly.

The fairy of the waters said nothing. She held out one slender, pearly hand, and Baradir placed the begrimed bottle into it. The glass dissolved into sand the moment her fingers touched it, and something pale and glimmering darted away.

'Foolish, the young,' she remarked. 'Most of my children remain within the walls of my garden. Those who stir beyond...' She did not finish the sentence, but she did not need to.

'I acquired it from a trader,' he offered. 'I do not think he knew what it was that he had.'

'But you did?' Her oceanic eyes regarded him with a limpid curiosity, but no anger.

'A suspicion only.'

'And how came you by this suspicion?'

Baradir hesitated. 'I am old, lady,' he said. 'I have — seen much.'

'There is power in you.'

To this observation, Baradir merely inclined his head.

'Not such as once there was,' she added, and slipping off her fountain perch, she drifted nearer. 'Something not of your weaving is there, also.' She stretched out that slender hand once more, and her fingertips brushed Baradir's chest, directly over his heart.

Baradir recoiled, for her touch was as ice. 'Please—' he began.

'Have you no heart?' she said in wonder.

What answer could he give, save the truth? 'No,' he softly said.

'How came you to lose it?'

He swallowed. 'That — I lost it through my own deeds, lady. I do not ask for sympathy.'

'Nor shall you receive any,' she said, but without rancour; absently, her attention only half upon Baradir's utterances. Her seawater gaze swept over Baradir, head to toe. 'Shall you ever have it back?'

He did not ask how it was that she came to understand the nature of his affliction, nor the century-long quest that had never, as yet, borne fruit. The truth, again, rose unbidden to his lips. 'I think not.'

'And what will become of you?' She looked into his eyes, reading them, unquenchably curious.

'I shall no longer be as other men are.'

'And when was the last time you were — as other men are?'

A pertinent question. It had not taken the freezing of his heart into glass to alter him thus; he had left the path of men behind long before.

This, he could not bring himself to say aloud.

'I do not like you,' she said, wonderingly.

Baradir, flayed by her words and the cool indifference of her cold-water gaze, flinched. 'I do not deserve your esteem,' he allowed, though the words emerged through a throat as dry as sand.

'Yet, you are the most interesting thing to wander into my garden in some time.'

'I—'

'That eye,' she said, interrupting him, one thin finger pointing unerringly at the eye lost to the sorcerous glass. 'What do you see through this eye?'

Baradir closed his enchanted eye. Through the other, still human, still ordinary, he saw only a woman. Beautiful to be sure, and perhaps a little fey, but no more than that. When he closed his healthy eye and opened the other, all her ancient magic was restored to his gaze: the pearly shimmer to her skin, the splintered ice in her hair, the depths of the seas shining out of her eyes.

He opened his mouth to express some of this, but found, once again, that he did not have to. Somehow, she saw it.

'I will help you,' she breathed.

Baradir went still. Well did he know that the "help" of a great power often proved more of a curse. 'Lady—' he began.

Too late. She closed the little remaining distance between them, and Baradir found himself engulfed. Her arms wound around him, drawing him to her; her hair spilled in slippery tendrils over his hands; her lips, cool as the rain and burning with heat, met his. She was snowfall and starlight and the deep cold of the desert after dark; yet also she was sunglow and warm waters, and the clear light of a burning moon. She held him to her for a time unknowable, and he felt his soul drown in freezing, sunlit waters.

Baradir, his senses in chaos, reeled.

When at last she stepped back, Baradir knew himself irrevocably changed.

'Thank you for returning my child,' she said, with an echo of formality.

Baradir stared, silenced, for every trace of the ordinary about her was gone. He no longer saw a mortal woman before him, not with his enchanted eye. He saw the fairy of the waters in all her power. If she had glimmered with ancient magic before, now she blazed with it. Sea mist wreathed a form scarcely feminine at all, for she was a fluid creature, water at its purest.

Her garden was altered, also. Drowned in water, or so it seemed, though it was *not* water, for he could breathe with every comfort. But the blossoms and foliage around him swayed and rippled as though tossed by watery currents, and the air shimmered with a liquid haze.

When he looked back at the fairy of the waters, he found her faded to nothing. Only her laughter echoed upon the air, at once delighted and mocking.

Baradir shut his treacherous eyes.

'I thank you for your help, lady,' he said, and managed to utter the words with only a hint of bitterness.

A current of air swirled past his face like the touch of warm water, and a doorway shimmered into life before him. He would not, he thought, have been able to see it with any clarity at all, only ten minutes before, for it was incorporeal, a weaving borne of the water-fairy's sorcery. Now it blazed in his vision, a pointed archway of river water and moonlight. He could discern nothing of what lay beyond.

'Farewell, then,' he sighed. Gathering his camels and his courage, he stepped through.

3

Beyond the arcane door, Baradir found a silent, starlit landscape. Sand dunes stretched as far as his altered eyes could see, pale in the moonlight. A mist wafted hither and thither, clinging to the ground, its airy contours aglow with some ancient sorcery. At first Baradir thought himself sent from one place of ethereal wonder to another, and bent his efforts to discovering which sorcerous realm the fairy of the waters had dispatched him to.

At length, when nothing more marvellous than the mists met his eye, and he had trudged some way over the starlit sands without encountering anything of note, it occurred to him that he had sought for too marvellous an explanation. He was returned into his own, familiar world; what he saw with his ensorcelled eyes was only the magic of the earth and the sky and the night — or perchance the remnants of an old enchantment, performed upon this spot on some long-past day.

An aching cold seeped into his bones, borne upon the night winds. The icy chill where his heart should be faded in comparison, came to seem almost warm. He walked on, but no alteration appeared to offer him hope, or to orient him. Empty, hushed night engulfed him, and seemed to go on forever.

Baradir stopped. What use in walking, with nowhere to go? His three camels gathered into a disconsolate knot around him as he stood in futile thought, deprived of the smallest inspiration. With what purpose had the fairy sent him here? Had she had any at all, or had she tossed him away with the carelessness of a child weary of a toy?

The latter was altogether too likely, Baradir thought — and then froze, for distantly upon the horizon a mote of colour shone. Crimson, vermillion, cobalt, emerald... colour and light winked in the distance like stars, tantalising, inviting.

Baradir stood frozen, thoughts awhirl. Those hues. Bejewelled, with the clarity of the finest gems — or of ensorcelled glass.

Familiar.

Slowly, he covered his left eye — blessed, or cursed, with fairy magic — and looked again.

The firmament was dark as pitch, unleavened by so much as a flicker of colour. A faint glow, that was all, easily dismissed as naught but a bright star.

His heart leapt.

Long he had searched, long and *long,* unaware that not even his sorcerous glass had the power to see *this* errant treasure with any clarity. Not if it sought to hide itself from him.

But little could hide from the arcane weavings of the fairy of the waters.

He stood, both eyes open, gazing his fill of the colours on the horizon. He saw the suggestion of a pair of minarets rising into the sky, outlined in light; and a great ogee dome between them, daubed in jewel-bright hues. As he looked, some new sensation eased his crystalline heart; or something old, unfelt for so many years he had ceased to recognise it.

Relief, he thought. Hope.

Then the colours were gone, fading away into the velvet night like a snuffed lamp.

'No!' he gasped, and with a curse, he leapt for Fasee's saddle. Sorcerer and caravan tore through the night, aiming unerringly for the remembered echoes of those taunting jewel-like shades. But, run though he might, stare though he may, not another glimpse of promising light did he catch.

On and on Baradir journeyed, until the sun burst over the sands and the heat began to climb. Then, exhausted and dismayed, he stopped, and swung down from Fasee's back. His weary camel swayed, and lowered her head.

'Yes,' he sighed. 'We have failed, have we not? But even a glimpse, Fasee, is more than we have enjoyed in many years. Come now, we must think.'

Fasee indicated herself to be more interested in rest, by the expedient of lowering herself to the sand. Her sisters joined her, leaving Baradir alone still alert, heedless of the scorching heat building around him.

'We go back,' he announced at last, for the benefit of an audience mostly asleep. 'To the starlit streets, and Iskandar.' For now he had a new tool at his disposal, a new curse to torment him with hope and disappointment. What might he see at the Starlight Bazaar, through the water-fairy's glamour? And what might he hear, if he asked of jewel-light shining upon the horizon at night? Those tales he had heard, down the long years: of a sumptuous palace shining in the dark, and vanishing with the dawn. Always a glimpse, and from far away; he had never heard that anyone had managed to reach it, or had ever set foot in it. But no longer was he disposed to dismiss the tales as a common mirage.

Only later, when the demands of an empty belly and the morning's encroaching heat required him to abandon his ruminations upon the arcane, did he chance to look closely at Talee, Fasee and Hanee. Each of his loyal, staid beasts of burden appeared somewhat different in his fairy-touched vision. What he had, at distracted glance, taken for traces of ambient magic clinging to their tails and toes and winding about their legs no longer appeared as such. Fasee, affectionate Fasee, had unmistakeably an aura of enchantment all her own.

Indeed, when a scorching day passed at last and embracing night once again fell, all three camels developed a certain quality of the ethereal in his cursed sight. And a notion more incongruous he could scarcely imagine, for who could have foreseen that these simple creatures of his might labour, like him, under sorcery?

What manner of spell it might be that burdened his camels, Baradir could not have said. His sorcerous sight offered him neither insight nor knowledge: only a vision of an altered world, tangled in magic and arcane mystery.

Well, the mystery of his camels he would add to the long list of questions he must someday answer.

The Bazaar appeared next on the outskirts of Al-Kabes, a scant mile beyond the city's edge. The ancient white-walled city occupied a swell of a hill in the midst of a harsh, unforgiving terrain; beyond the walls, the ground was rocky, uneven, thick with vicious plants bristling with thorns. Only two roads led to Al-Kabes, or permitted passage out again, and these were hard-won, hacked through the landscape by sheer force of will. Twice a year, the encroaching wilds had to be cleared away from the narrow, winding roads between Al-Kabes and Parsas far to the north, or the walled city and the Nabbir river valley spreading to the south-east.

Upon this northern road, there lay concealed an alcove, hidden from the path behind two jagged boulders wreathed in thorns. Here Baradir waited as the sun set, seventeen days having passed since his encounter with the fairy. A scant two of these had he spent in the city, recovering from his long journey, and making what subtle enquiries he could of its residents.

No one had heard of an ensorcelled palace that vanished into thin air. Indeed, he received a great many searching looks for even asking such a question, and concluded that, in the days following his stay in Al-Kabes, he would be spoken of as a wandering madman.

'It would not be the first time, hm, Fasee?' he murmured, stroking her bristly nose. He could almost feel the sorcery rolling off her, now that he knew it was there, though the sensation must be only imagined.

He began a crooning lullaby for her amusement, and that of her sisters tucked against the jagged rock walls behind him. But he stopped singing abruptly when another traveller entered the alcove, a figure so bundled in kaftan and cloak and scarf that he could discern nothing of his or her appearance.

All serenity vanished, and Baradir tensed. He returned the stranger's nod civilly enough, but kept his distance.

'You are here for the Bazaar?' said the newcomer, and the voice was pitched low: male.

'Yes,' said Baradir.

The man nodded. 'Mazin bin Imad al-Salak,' he said, with a bow oddly courtly in spite of the bulk of his layers. 'I am a trader in wonders. Healing incense, and restorative elixirs! A phoenix egg here and there, if I can contrive it, and but *once* in my career, a Xingqing tea set. Those glasses filled themselves, my friend, with the finest of brews, and required naught to do so but sun and rain and wind. I was sorely tempted to keep it for myself, I can tell you, but when a man is given a chance at that kind of profit...' He shook his head, and bowed again. 'And what brings you to the Starlight Bazaars?'

'Information,' said Baradir, declining to offer his name. Many decades had passed since the name of Ibn Samar had been widely known, and widely notorious, but Yasmine had made him cautious. Somehow, the old tales of his deeds and misdeeds were surfacing again. 'You travel a great deal, I take it?' he said, before the man could press him for his identity.

'Oh, from the Jade Sea to the Pearl Coast, and every route and road in between! And for many years now.'

'Then perhaps you will have heard something of what I seek,' said Baradir. 'A great palace, built they say from sorcerous glass.'

Baradir felt himself scrutinised, but Mazin made as yet no answer.

'It is more likely to be glimpsed at night,' Baradir persevered. 'A distant presence on the far horizon, never to be reached, for it vanishes into the air.'

'A vanishing palace?' said Mazin.

'Yes,' said Baradir.

'Such a palace would be among the great wonders of this world.'

'It was,' said Baradir. 'Once. Perhaps it still is.'

Mazin was silent for some moments. 'There was an old tale about such a place,' he said after a time. 'They do not speak of it so much now, but when I was a child—'

'I seek recent information,' Baradir interrupted, for they seemed but half a breath from a tale of Ibn Samar, the wicked sorcerer.

'Oh, there is forever some new tale of a house, or a town, or a city, that beckons one with promises of plenty only to fade into the heat! Mirages are common in some parts of the world, my friend. You have the look of a seasoned traveller about you. You must know this.'

'I do not speak of mirages,' said Baradir.

Mazin was again silent. 'Only once did I hear a tale I thought might be more than a simple illusion,' he said. 'A woman in Sulanah—'

'*Sulanah*?' echoed Baradir.

'A woman in Sulanah spoke of a night-palace, all painted with colour. It was under the control of a great jinn, she said, who took it about with him as she herself might carry a basket, putting it down here and there as it pleased him, and taking it away with him as he chose. She was old, and her family thought her weak in the mind. But I wondered. She spoke of this night-palace almost as though she had seen it herself.'

'Sulanah,' said Baradir again. 'I thank you. I wonder—'

This new question remained unasked, for a great grinding of rock interrupted Baradir's words: the wall was opening, and light streamed from within. Light, and the perfume of night-blooming flowers; traces of incense upon the air, and the tantalising scents of wine and coffee and meat cooked in bright flames. Music caught at his heart, beckoning him inside.

He needed no urging, and nor did Mazin, who preceded Baradir into the Starlight Bazaar with alacrity and was soon lost in the crowd.

Baradir woke Hanee and Talee, and followed.

'Ah!' said a female voice which, sadly, he knew.

4

Baradir whirled, and found Yasmine seated cross-legged atop a tiny stool, just inside the Bazaar's entrance. She did not rise to intercept him, nor did she accost him with further words. But she watched him closely as he manoeuvred his camels inside the opening in the rock, and he did not like the look in her night-black eyes.

'What is it that you now want?' said Baradir, when she neither spoke nor went away.

'My wishes have not changed.'

'Nor has my answer.'

She held an ornate glass in her hand, an airy confection of moon-white shot through with azure. Whatever was in it gave off a tantalising aroma as she raised it to her lips and took a long swallow, quite large enough a draught to empty the vessel. But the scent of that beverage — roses and honey and pomegranate at least, and cinnamon and plum — did not fade, and when Baradir glanced again at the thing, it was still full with clear liquid. Yasmine savoured her drink, with an air of casual ease he liked no better than the contempt with which she beheld him. 'Do you never offer your aid to another, Ibn Samar?'

'You should not call me that.'

'Why not, if it is your name?'

'You choose to call it mine, but I have yet to own to it.' Baradir looked away, busied himself with unburdening Fasee and her sisters, and avoided Yasmine's gaze.

'Why have you come back,' said Yasmine, 'if it is not to assist me?'

'Surely you had not expected I would travel all this way at *your* beck and call.'

Her lip curled. 'And you deny that you are Ibn Samar.'

Baradir straightened. 'And have you sat here every night, waiting for me?'

'Yes,' Yasmine acknowledged. 'But I shan't do so again.'

'It would be useless.'

'So I see.' She rose from the stool, and shook out the draping folds of her cloak. What she did with her remarkable glass Baradir did not see, but it was no longer in her hands. 'I am Yasmine bint Izebadd,' she said formally, and made him obeisance, though there was mockery in the gestures of respect. Previously, Baradir had seen little out of the ordinary about her; a human woman she had seemed to him to be. But now, he saw her differently. Her brown skin contained a veritable torrent of arcane magic; the old kind. The dangerous kind.

'Izebadd,' he said, and drew back from her. 'That is an uncommon name.' A name he knew; but, surely, it could not be the same...

She smiled. 'I name you Ibn Samar, and I will claim your aid, doubt me not.'

He swallowed. 'Why must it be me? Why cannot another serve your purpose just as well?'

'It must be you,' was all she said. 'A pact? If you will help me, I will help you.'

'What are you?'

'An impertinence, to ask.'

'If you seek a pact, I would know with what I am bargaining.'

'Not unwise,' she conceded. 'You have heard, I think, of my father.'

Baradir swallowed, and would not answer.

'A pact, Ibn Samar.'

'I am *Baradir*.'

'Very well.'

'What do you imagine I need help with?'

'You are looking for your palace, aren't you?'

He stared.

'A wondrous creation; I applaud your skill. And built without even the assistance of a jinn, do they not say? No wonder your name was spoken ten kingdoms over.'

A jinn. Those words from her lips pierced his defences, forced him to recall. A tale of danger and daring, some hundred years ago; of a girl, Sabira al-Raad, and the jinn called Izebadd…

He swallowed. 'Was your mother's name Sabira, Yasmine bint Izebadd?'

She laughed, and made him obeisance more sincere than those that had gone before. 'You are quick, Baradir.'

'Daughter of the jinn, *what do you want with me*?'

'I have told you.'

'And I do not believe it. If you are the daughter of Izebadd, you cannot be in need of anyone's help. Least of all mine.'

'There are some things beyond the reach of my power, Ibn Samar. And even my father's.'

He stilled at that, and his heart beat quick, for her words implied that *he*, and his palace, were numbered among those rarefied things.

'I know better than to tangle with the jinn,' he said, and backed farther away from her.

'And I ought to know better than to tangle with a heartless sorcerer, but I will do as I must.'

'I have no need of your aid.' He bowed, and withdrew, seeking to lose himself in the crowd as quickly as he might.

'You will never find your palace without me,' she called after him. 'You'll see.'

Baradir did not choose to reply.

<hr>

Later, he sat alone and disconsolate under the crimson awnings of a wine-tent, making inroads upon his fifth cup of pomegranate wine. He had been well accustomed to such heady libations, once, and could have dispatched bottles of the stuff before he felt any deleterious effects. Now, he could no longer say the same. A mere few cups, and his head was thick and aching, his thoughts as slow as poured sugar-syrup, and the world turned if he was so unwise as to stand up.

He rather preferred the state to what had gone before.

He'd left Yasmine, plunging into the Bazaar's crowds of traders and revellers in perfect confidence that he would soon lose himself among them; that he would find his way back to the relative peace, the peculiar kind of safety and anonymity, that came from being merely one face among many. The Bazaar had always offered him solace before. He would eat, and drink, and trade some of his pack-goods, and he would talk to some of the many people here who had no notion of who he was. Iskandar, too, if he could find him.

He had reckoned without the water-fairy's interference. If he had seen magic roiling off Yasmine in waves, even shrouding something so ordinary and familiar (he had thought) as his camels, what might he see at the Bazaar? The thought may have crossed his mind, but he had been in no way prepared for what awaited him there.

Little proved mundane at a Starlight Bazaar. Every man, woman and child he met rippled with magic; it wound around their hands and feet, washed over their backs like tattered cloaks, shone in their eyes with a weird, intense radiance. Some few of them were — worse. Like Yasmine, they were human enough to an unseeing eye, but he saw their true faces beneath the glamour of an ordinary appearance. He saw the sorcery that poured off them in waves, seeping into everything they touched.

When half the wares that changed hands were soaked in enchantment, and even some of the dishes Baradir might once have imbibed betrayed a more than passing acquaintance with the arcane, well, he was unequal to it. Everywhere he looked, sorcery; everything he touched, magic; it surged and flickered and flared and dazzled until Baradir was sick and fevered and dizzy, overwhelmed and (in his heart of hearts) afraid.

For he wondered. Through his ensorcelled left eye, he had begun to see all this already. Mere traces compared to the flood unleashed by the fairy's curse, to be sure, but what if she had not simply bestowed this sight upon him? What if she had merely accelerated a process already begun?

Was this what he was destined to become? Nothing left of *him* but sorcery; magic was all he would ever see, magic all he would ever be again. Magic twisted. Magic gone wrong.

Like many a man before him, he sought refuge in his cups, and found them comforting. At least *this* beverage boasted no unusual properties to dazzle his eyes; a good, simple pomegranate wine, and nothing more.

He ordered another cup.

'Baradir, my friend!' came a hearty roar at his ear, and Iskandar materialised. He found it necessary, the bear, to beat Baradir upon the back in enthusiastic welcome, making him choke. 'Another of whatever this fellow is having,' he said to the vendor, and upon its appearance downed half of its contents in two swallows.

Only then did he take a close look at Baradir.

'Have I ever seen you intoxicated?' he mused. 'Before today, that is.'

'No,' said Baradir.

'And what could ruffle the implacable composure of Baradir bin Samar, I wonder?' Iskandar took the stool next to Baradir. The jewels in his beard were clear white, today, and they shone with such a piercing light — like stars, far too close and achingly bright — that Baradir's eyes watered, and he shut them. His head spun.

'Well,' said Iskandar conversationally. 'Did you know there's a woman claiming Ibn Samar is here at the Bazaar, tonight? Is that perhaps it?'

'No,' said Baradir again, and sighed. 'Though it doesn't help.' What was Yasmine about now? If she thought to compel his assistance by exposing his identity, she had missed her mark. All he would do was run.

Again.

'Whatever it is, I do not think drinking will help,' said Iskandar helpfully, and punctuated this wisdom by draining the contents of his own wine-cup, and instantly requesting another.

'I do not think it will, either,' said Baradir. 'Until I render myself prone and oblivious for the rest of the night, and such is my intention.'

'With the whole Bazaar talking of you?'

'No one will believe her. Those stories are a hundred years old.'

'But remembered, for all of that.'

Baradir set his empty cup down with a snap. 'Iskandar. Did you come here to add to my woes?'

Iskandar's eyes twinkled. 'You are truly awful company in the grip of self-pity, my friend.'

'I am truly awful company, in any condition. Whatever it was that brought you here tonight, pray get on with it.'

'I have news.'

Baradir sat up a little straighter. 'Of?'

'Your wandering abode, I think.'

Here he paused, and took a lingering sip of wine.

Baradir's hands clenched into fists. 'Iskandar, if you do not wish to have your neck wrung, say on. And quickly.'

'What would you say if I told you that it is in Sulanah?'

'I would say it is the second time this night I've heard of such a connection. Though the first came by way of a senile old woman, and was at least second-hand information at that.'

Iskandar at once turned wary. 'Quite the coincidence.'

'Yes, is it not?'

'And with that woman about…' Iskandar did not need to elaborate on who he meant. He shrugged. 'I made my usual enquiries, earlier this evening, and heard two tales of your vanishing palace from two separate sources. Both named your birth-city, and claimed recent sightings, too. Make of that what you will.'

'That is too many coincidences.'

'You think it is a trap?'

'I think that Yasmine has been laying clues for me.'

Iskandar looked curiously. 'Who is this Yasmine?'

'Yasmine bint Izebadd.'

Iskandar whistled. 'What have you done to earn her ire?'

'She wants something from me.'

'And?'

'I said no.'

Iskandar shook his head. 'You are right, my friend,' he said, and clapped Baradir on the back. 'You are truly awful company. It's my suggestion you don't stay at the Bazaar tonight.'

'I've nowhere else to go.'

'No? What of that wondrous tent of yours?'

'Nearly spent.'

'Then,' said Iskandar, 'it's my suggestion that you stop drinking.' He winked at the wine vendor, said, 'Don't give him any more, all right?'

Then, with a brief obeisance to Baradir, Iskandar took himself off.

Baradir watched as his friend's bulky figure disappeared into the swell of people beyond the wine-vendor's tent.

Baradir became aware of the scrutiny of his nearest neighbours. True, some several feet separated him from his fellow drinkers; he had chosen this particular spot with care. But, Iskandar did not always understand how penetrating was his voice.

Somewhere beneath the haze of sorcery shrouding those figures, he detected suspicion.

With regret, he plunged his face one last time into his wine-cup, revelling in the fragrance that filled his nose, and the flood of sweet, intoxicating wine over his tongue.

Then he set the cup down, shouldered his bundle of wares, and went in search of Fasee, Hanee and Talee.

He would not to go Sulanah. *You will never find your palace without me,* Yasmine had said, and now here was a clear trail set out for him to follow, purporting to lead him straight there. He had not spent a century in the search without learning a thing or two. Such elusive information did not conveniently fall into one's lap, and all in a single day.

It had to be Yasmine's doing.

What alternative did he have? He had the evidence of his own eyes, and his own recent experience — of which, he trusted, Yasmine could know nothing.

He had seen his lost palace himself, not long ago. And it had been nowhere near Sulanah.

How had he contrived it? Through the water-fairy's interference, yes — but it had been his own, wondrous tent that had taken him there.

It had sometimes occurred to him to wonder whether his tent's doors (such as they were) opened upon wide-flung locations truly at random. Was it only chance, or was there some twist to its ancient sorcery that made it something more?

Had the water-fairy's child manipulated its magic, as he had first assumed? Had his tent opened upon the fairy's garden through the sprite's will?

Or had it done so because it was where he most needed to go at that moment? Where he and the sprite *both* had needed to go?

Perhaps it was time to test the truth of this idea. Now that he had the eyes to see, perhaps it was time, at long last, for his tent to deliver him home.

If not... well, though he did not often like to hazard the use of his own arts, he need not consider himself reduced to a wholly magicless condition. Perhaps he might... *encourage* the tent to do as he wished.

5

HAVING REFRESHED HIMSELF, AND in some degree moderated his rash drunkenness, with a large jug of ice-water-and-rose, Baradir extricated himself from the Bazaar. He did so by the simple expedient of keeping his treacherous eyes shut as much as possible, or nearly so, employing just enough of his cursed vision to manoeuvre a way through the milling crowds and the rings of tents. Still, he arrived at the exit with streaming eyes and his thoughts in disarray, and had just presence of mind enough to note that Yasmine had abandoned her perch by the rock-door.

He was not again accosted by her, nor by anyone else. Perhaps the scarf he had wound over his head had helped to conceal any distinguishing features Yasmine might have taken it upon herself to spread around. He did, though, hear more than one voice utter his name as he threaded through the throng. *Ibn Samar, Ibn Samar...*

To think that he had once *sought* such notoriety.

He slipped through the rock opening as unobtrusively as he could, guiding his loyal camels through, and upon finding himself restored to the tranquillity of a quiet night, and a soothing darkness unleavened by too many untoward flashes of magic, he permitted himself a long sigh of relief.

He was weary. His head ached with a stabbing pain behind his eyes, and his steps were heavy as he trailed back out into the road. Desperately he wanted rest; but it would not do to open his ensorcelled bundle of cloth here, when anybody might come upon him at any moment. Such a treasure as he had was worth killing for, however scant few folds it had left. Came it to such a battle, it would not be *he* paying for it with his life.

Grimly, he gripped Fasee, Hanee and Talee's ropes and re-traced his steps into Al-Kabes. He had not yet relinquished his room there. Its proportions, though not handsome, ought to be sufficient to accommodate his tent.

He was on the point of passing through the city gates when he found himself, at last, accosted. The great wooden structures beckoned, tall shapes outlined against a starry sky, but before Baradir could put more than one foot over the threshold, a weight barrelled into him from somewhere behind, and he went sprawling into the dirt of the road.

'Ibn Samar,' snarled a voice. Baradir saw naught of its owner save an indistinct figure roiling with the darkfire of sorcery. Sparks exploded around his clenched fists; a sorcerer, and he had felled Baradir with a spell.

'I am not he,' croaked Baradir, tensed and waiting. He did not choose, yet, to rise, but lay watchful.

'The jinn's daughter says otherwise.' His hands moved, and Baradir tensed, awaiting the impact of another lancing spell.

Instead, he felt an insistent force coiling about his ankles and his wrists, forcing his feet together, his hands to meet behind his back. Another such force crept over his lips, seeking to silence him.

Anger blossomed in Baradir's breast.

'The jinn's daughter knows nothing of the case,' he snarled. 'Ibn Samar died long ago. There is nothing left of him now.' That, honesty compelled him to admit, was not quite the truth; traces of Ibn Samar's character still surfaced in him, even now. Tonight was bidding fair to prove one of those regrettable occasions. 'Leave be, boy,' he growled. 'You know not what you do.'

'I will rid the world of a pestilence,' said the sorcerer, and his voice, nay, the very righteousness of his words, proved his youth. He was no inconsiderable talent; his sorcery held Baradir bound fast, and in a posture primed to receive a killing blow straight to his worthless glass heart.

Baradir did not struggle. He sought to meet the boy's eyes in the darkness, but could not find them. 'Let me go,' he said, more softly, but in a tone which rang with authority.

'No.' The sorcerer — so, so young! And so sure of the very rightness of all he did! — raised a hand. His fingers bore rings of great arcane power, two of them; they flared to life in Baradir's sight, colouring the air with magic.

'I beseech you,' said Baradir in some desperation, swallowing his pride. 'Do not make me—'

The boy was not listening. He unleashed his spell, a killing wave designed to carry Baradir straight out of life.

Ibn Samar had weathered many such attacks before, long years ago. Baradir bin Samar, changed though he was, well remembered the tricks and arts he had once employed to win every conflict in which he found himself. He had slain every challenger to his supremacy, left every righteous hero in pieces behind him. He might, now, have stayed his hand, and softened the impact of his countering sorcery. He need not kill the boy, after all; he only needed a little space in which to escape.

Alas, his body remembered. His magic knew the way. Before he knew what he was about, habit had taken care of the matter for him. The boy's own sorcery twisted away from Baradir, repelled by sheer force of superior might, and rebounded upon its caster, shocking him motionless. And in that instant, a tendril of Baradir's own magic snaked out, caught the boy's throat in a paralysing grip, and crushed the life out of him.

It took, perhaps, three seconds.

Baradir lay, shaken and breathless, as the hapless boy's spells dissolved, restoring his freedom of movement. His own magic ebbed away in its wake, and his anger with it, leaving him empty.

He drew himself to his feet, and stood looking down upon the slain form of his youthful foe. The boy had never had a chance. Considering the utter certainty with which he had approached Baradir, never doubting for a second his true, and terrible, identity — what had possessed him to attack like that? Had it been pure arrogance, to think that he could so easily best so notoriously powerful a sorcerer?

Whatever had moved him, it had ended as such battles always did: with another corpse at Baradir's feet, another burden upon his soul, another weight upon his fractured glass heart. As he stood grappling with his regrets, rigid with a renewed anger directed now at *himself*, he felt a stiffening and the insidious creep of ice somewhere inside his chest.

When next he had courage enough to seek the company of a mirror, and without the glamour that hid the encroaching curse under which he lived, Baradir knew he'd see a change. He'd lost another skirmish with himself; some part of his body would pay for it. Next time he looked in the mirror, he would be lesser in warmth, in flesh, in humanity; greater in the brittle chill of glass.

'Well,' said Baradir heavily, and turned his back upon the fallen sorcerer. 'I've deserved it.'

When he passed at last through the beckoning gate of Al-Kabes, he moved with the weary gait of an old, old man, for once feeling every one of his years.

Baradir found his rooms as he had left them: empty, and silent. But he could no longer draw any peace from the absence of people, or of magic. The stillness came at odds with the conflicts raging in his heart, and for an absurd instant he longed for the bustle and chaos of the Bazaar he had been in such a hurry to leave. Had it only been an hour ago?

He forced such thoughts from his mind, and adjured himself to think clearly. What did he need? His tent. Yes. He'd taken a room on the ground floor of a shabby inn, so insalubrious a place that the proprietor had no stable in which to house Baradir's camels, nor any objection to his housing them in his own room instead. He'd learned, over the years, that wisdom lay in keeping his friends — and his hard-won goods — close, and what matter if the latter were beasts of burden?

If they were. He sourly regarded the glimmer of magic around Fasee as she bumped her nose against his stomach, and sucked up the sweet dates he offered her.

Too many mysteries. What must a man give for a life of peace?

This thought, too, he banished, and having distributed a similar largesse to Fasee's sisters, he retrieved his bundle of folded cloth from deep within one of Talee's packs. Without giving himself time to regret its diminished state, nor to think too long upon the limited uses of its powers now left to him, he loosed another fold in the cloth. To his interest, a torrent of magic diffused into the air, unleashed with the drawing-back of the cloth. It spread into all the corners of his room, a hazy, half-glimpsed mist that turned everything indistinct.

Then he could see it no longer, for the silk leapt out of his hands and began to grow. It grew and grew, throwing out length after length of cloth, until a riot of woven colours had taken the place of the drab, shabby little room, and a handsome tent stood proudly before him.

Two panels drew back; a door appeared, beckoning Baradir inside; and in he went.

Inside, it no longer much resembled a tent.

Before, he had always seen cloth — sumptuous cloth, to be sure, of the finest silks, and in every imaginable hue, but cloth nonetheless. The sorcery that powered his tent, he supposed, had camouflaged itself as such, and his mind had been happy to go along with the illusion.

Now, not a scrap of woven fibre could he discern. The tent was a mass of magic, a cocoon of the stuff to cradle a sorcerer inside. The colours were still there, if anything more brilliant than before; but the structure was incorporeal, an effusion of arcane light that could not but dazzle his poor eyes if looked upon too long.

Still, that made the task at hand a little easier.

He was intrigued to note, in passing, that the array to some degree resembled a structure of airy, colour-stained glass.

He settled his camels, with a dish of water each and a stock of fruit, for he did not know how long it might be before he could tend to them again. This done, he shut his smarting eyes, reached out his hands, and felt for the sorcery all around him with those senses to which no one had ever put a satisfactory name. How was it that he could feel the arcane power surrounding him, though he could not touch it, or smell it, taste it or — in the ordinary way of things — see it? What strange, sixth sense permitted him to discern the shape of the spell, to grasp at it, manipulate it, coax it into some new configuration that suited him better?

He could not have said with what voice he spoke to the spell, nor with what understanding it accepted his instructions and bent itself to perform them. He only knew that, when he had finished, the "tent" knew him for its master, leapt to obey his commands.

Baradir took a moment to reflect. To work sorcery unsettled him, nowadays. It had never been so, before; not until the events which had twisted his magics, turned them upon *him,* Ibn Samar, in the worst of ways, and fractured his life forever. Since then, he had never known quite what might happen when he called upon his old arts.

He did not know what would happen now.

Summoning his nerve — and endeavouring *not* to think of the last use to which he had put these same arts, and the cooling corpse he'd left behind in the process — Baradir opened his lips and, in the old tongue, he said: 'When I depart this tent, you will deliver me to the place where my palace resides.'

Something in the tent's sorcerous make-up shifted and re-wove itself, settling into a new pattern. Acknowledgement enough, Baradir thought. Sorely tempted was he to exit the tent at once, and see where he came out, but he refrained.

He told himself it was a matter of good sense. The hour was late, he was weary, and an interval of rest and slumber would benefit him greatly before he embarked upon the task of finding, and reclaiming, his palace.

A small voice, somewhere at the back of his mind, babbled in fear, but went unacknowledged. Baradir would not think of the disasters that might lie on the horizon tomorrow; nor would he remember those last, terrible days in his beloved palace, before he had fled, and lost himself in the desert.

He was a different man now.

Wrapping himself in his precious Xingqing blankets, Baradir bin Samar put all disquieting thoughts from his well-practiced mind and drifted into sleep.

⁂

He woke in the night.

For some time he lay frozen, his heart unaccountably pounding, his forehead chilly with a sheen of sweat. When nothing untoward occurred, and nothing that did not belong met his searching gaze, he was moved to put his condition down to some nightmare of his own mind's fashioning, forgotten the moment he left his state of slumber.

But then the colours in the ethereal walls shifted, and formed patterns. Images.

Stories.

Baradir watched, more in fascination than alarm, as a vision of his own, precious palace formed before his eyes. There was the arched dome over which he had laboured; the tall minarets; the vast double doors firmly closed against the world. A dwelling fit for a sultan.

And there, looming over this miniature vision of perfection, was Baradir's own face as it had once been. Young. To Baradir's weary eyes, so absurdly, painfully youthful. Far more handsome than had ever been good for him, his hair and beard black and thick. Everything about that face repelled Baradir now: the contemptuous twist to his smile, the arrogance of his stance, the very *satisfaction* — with himself, with his life, his power — that shone from his hard black eyes.

As Baradir watched in growing revulsion, the desert sands surged and dipped beneath his marvellous palace of wonders. The edifice wavered, and toppled, and disappeared, vanishing in a roar of sand.

But that isn't what happened, he thought numbly, and was obliged to watch as the scene repeated itself all over again. Only this time, it was arcane flame that doomed his creation, devouring it in an inferno of blue fire. And the next time, a great jinn — an afreet — opened his mouth and swallowed the palace whole.

The scenes went on and on, and each time the palace of Ibn Samar met its end by some new disaster.

Baradir, frozen for some time in horror, abruptly shook himself, and barrelled out of the warmth of his enfolding blankets. Nightmares indeed, doubtless dreamed up by his own recalcitrant brain — and had he not taken pains to ensure the wondrous tent would carry out his will? Had he not set its workings to focus upon his lost palace? Here was an unintended consequence.

He need not stay for the rest of the performance.

Working with haste, he retrieved his pack of necessities only, and left his trade-goods where they lay. Senseless to burden the camels with wares he would have no means of bartering away. When the three camels were roused and on their feet, and Baradir himself dressed in all his layers of sirwal and mantle and robe, he made straight for the door without pausing to think, commanded it to open, and stepped out into the unknown.

Six steps beyond, he stopped and stood rooted in astonishment. For the sight that met his anxious eyes informed him that the tent had taken him far beyond its usual boundaries.

Little of the corporeal he saw, and nothing of the ordinary. A landscape of utter madness lay spread before him. The terrain was a desert, a mass of sands that shifted and dipped and surged as he watched. This had proved no obstacle for the construction of dwelling-places, for he saw two structures built upon this unstable ground, each highly curious in design, erupting with spires and domes in peculiar places, and seeming undecided as to their proportions or size. A third attracted his eye, farther out, all but disappearing below the horizon.

They were wrought from the same substance as his tent: neither stone nor wood, indeed nothing so practical, but sorcery woven in its purest form into flights of the strangest fancy.

Baradir stared, and realisation dawned, even as his breath caught in his throat and something like panic (or anger, or wonder) shredded his composure into tatters.

He no longer walked the lands of men. The tent had delivered him to those realms belonging to creatures fantastic and (to most) invisible.

And the specific part to which he was come could only be the lands of the jinn.

6

Faithless, contorted magic! Baradir wasted some time in bitter rumination upon his corrupted arts. Of what use was it to be a sorcerer if one's spells always went awry, and were reliable only in their tendency to land one in a worse situation than that from which one would like to escape? He kicked furiously at the sand-like substance beneath his feet — sand in semblance only, for his feet met with nothing of any great solidity, and his attempts to abuse it met with no satisfying *thunk*, no cathartic spray of sand into the air.

At length he collected his temper, and his scattered wits besides, and could look about himself with greater sense.

Unexpected destination. He'd imagined himself likely to emerge somewhere in the Silversands, the pale desert in which the water-fairy had dumped him before. If not that, well, perhaps Sulanah, for there was always the possibility that one or two of those stories of palace-sightings had some truth to them.

He was far-flung indeed, as far as he had ever been from those familiar lands. And if he mistook not, the realm to which he had come was nowhere he might wish to linger. Jinni were capricious creatures, of limitless power, and known for sometimes mad whims. It surprised him not at all, therefore, to note the unpromising quality to the glowering sky, or the arcane storms hanging heavy on the wind-tossed horizon. Fanciful those dwellings might be, but the air held a quality of menace, a sense of pressure and dire foreboding. Did Baradir sense these things with his eyes or his skin, or was it his sorcerer's sense that warned him of danger were he to linger too long?

He turned in a circle, casting a long, considering look over the landscape in every direction. He saw nothing to mitigate his unease. Nothing looked as it ought, to Baradir's human notions. The sands underfoot were black in parts, or the purple colour of an old bruise, or the blue of a stormy twilight; everything but yellow, or orange, or white. The sky mimicked these effects, or perhaps it was the other way around, for great mountainous clouds dominated the firmament, one or two a reassuring shade of white with silver shining about them, but the rest all purpling with fury and poised to unleash the veriest hell at any moment.

Baradir did not, as yet, notice any jinni about, and thought it desirable to remove himself from their home before he had the misfortune to run into any.

But when he retrieved his wrapped bundle of cloth, and had occasion to observe how thin it had become, he discovered to his horror that a single, useful fold remained. One scant, precious pocket of magic with which to summon his marvellous tent; once used, the contraption would be lost to him, together with all its contents.

He hesitated.

Yes, his need was dire — though, was it? He was come to a place of danger, true, but no immediate danger threatened.

What if he used up this last wisp of sorcery, and found himself, at some future date, far more urgently in need of rescue? With what regret he would *then* look back on this day, and wish he had been stouter of heart.

He put the bundle away.

'After all,' he observed to Fasee, who, suffering some unease of her own, huddled close to him. 'We are in the land of the jinni, and might that not be seen rather as opportunity than disaster? For who else could transport me, in the blink of an eye, back to the realms of men? And who else could find my palace for me, Fasee, with the greatest of ease, and without the smallest delay? Yasmine boasted of such power, but she forgot that there is more to the world of jinni than herself and her father.' So saying, Baradir heartened himself, and resolved upon attempting a meeting with some one or other of the jinn.

It would not be his first time treating with their number. He knew what he was about.

So said he, warm in the glow of confidence. But not three steps did he travel before the shadowy sand underfoot unaccountably rose up to engulf him, and he discovered himself to be, not purposefully striding over it as he'd intended, but face down in it. Prone.

It clung to him, imparting a creeping chill to his shrinking limbs which set him a-shiver.

He lifted his head, spitting damp sand (or something that felt much like it), and beheld a jinn standing before him.

Standing, no. Floating three feet above the ground, and therefore towering far over Baradir in his recumbent posture. The jinn's form was only loosely that of a man, for he had the head of a great desert fox, and clawed paws to match. He appeared as insubstantial as the plane that had produced him, and instead of garments of cloth or wool he wore a swirling... robe, it must be called, of glittering sand tossed by the winds of an arcane storm. The breezes it emitted reached Baradir even so far below, sweeping back his hair and setting his teeth on edge.

The jinn was, incidentally, immense.

'Well,' said Baradir, hauling himself up from his humiliating position. It had never been any part of his intention to *grovel* before these beings. 'I bid you good day.' He made obeisance, choosing by way of precaution to make it a very low one, full of respect.

'How came you here?' said the jinn.

'How?' said Baradir. 'By sorcery. How else?'

The jinn digested this. 'You are a sorcerer.'

'Can you not see my nature written upon my features, as I can discern yours?'

The jinn, to Baradir's discomfort, drifted nearer, and bent down its fox-head, nose working to snuffle up every hint of... scent? 'I smell sorcery on you,' he conceded.

'That is because I am filled to the brim with it.' Baradir smiled, with what he hoped was a show of confidence. They were like beasts, these jinni; to show fear could prove fatal, but present yourself as an equal, or better yet a superior, and—

The earth flew up to smack Baradir in the face, and he received a mouthful of the moist, foul stuff. He had the curious impression that he had not fallen face-first into it, as might appear; he had experienced no sensation of falling, nor had he suffered much impact. Rather, it was as though the earth itself had tipped up and collided with his face.

Either way, he was once again prone.

'I smell dishonour on you, also,' said the jinn, not with menace, but with grave disapproval, as though Baradir had been a once-favoured son who had proved disappointing.

Baradir spat out dirt, and raised himself up to his knees. 'And have you never committed a dishonourable act?'

'A jinn does not explain himself to a man.'

'A man need not explain himself to a jinn, either.' Baradir succeeded in gaining his feet again, and stood in imminent expectation of receiving another faceful of earth.

'He does when he has conveyed himself, uninvited, to the jinn's lands.'

'And for that I apologise,' said Baradir, with another obeisance. 'I had in fact sought a different destination, and have come here by mistake.'

'Your sorcery, then, is nothing to boast of.' The jinn folded huge, bulky arms, and drifted a fraction higher.

Words of denial rose to Baradir's lips, and died away again. How could he deny it? 'Again, I apologise,' he said instead.

The jinn's head tilted. 'Where were you trying to go, little sorcerer?'

'My destination lies in the lands of men,' said Baradir, swallowing his indignant objection to the word *little*. 'I would never have set foot in your august realms by intention.'

The jinn waved this away. 'Your error is established. Nonetheless, you trespass.'

'I do, and I would like to cease doing so as soon as possible. If you would lend me your aid—'

'You ask a boon?' The disapproval grew deeper, and into the jinn's tone crept a hint, at last, of menace.

'A small one,' Baradir persevered, bracing himself. 'If you could send me to the place I was attempting to reach, I would by the same means be removed from your lands.'

'You shall certainly be removed from these lands,' said the jinn, and unfolded his arms.

Baradir took this as a bad sign. Did he mean to banish the interloper with a flick of his finger? Where might a lone sorcerer end up?

'A palace,' said Baradir desperately. 'A marvel wrought of glass, in every colour there is. It once stood at the pinnacle of the great mountain, Marikalat, and in those days it was the home of— of a great sorcerer. It is not there now, but if you can find out where it has gone, and send me there—'

The jinn never said another word in Baradir's hearing. A terrible smile stretched across his fox's head of a face, baring his sharp teeth. Then, with the careless gesture Baradir had been every moment dreading, he sent Baradir sailing out of his lands.

A blink, and a breath, and Baradir found himself...

...in another nonsensical landscape, half of it drenched in the blistering heat of a burning sun, the other half lashed with the winds and rains of an unnatural storm. The division between the two was a clear, hard line; not a drop of rain crossed it into the opposing landscape, nor did so much as a single stray beam of sunlight wander into the storm. It was as two distinct worlds set edge-to-edge by some whim of a god — or, as Baradir thought more likely, a jinn.

Two jinni, perhaps, for an ornate palace stood in each realm: a tower of onyx, white and black, stood tall in the one, its gleaming walls untouched by the rain. An edifice of clouds and light hung over the other, drifting far above the ground, though a stair of spiralling cloud-stuff wound down from above.

Baradir, to his disgust, emerged in the storm-tossed half. His three camels, more fortunate souls, appeared in the heat and sun opposite. Only some four or five feet away from Baradir they might be, but the conditions *they* enjoyed could not have been farther removed.

He could have sworn there was a smug look on Talee's face.

To his greater dismay, he was demonstrably still in the lands of the jinn. His challenger hadn't removed him from the jinn-lands at all. Considering his disapproval of Baradir's trespass, he must intend some mischief by sending him into this odd land of opposites, and it would behove Baradir to remove himself from it as soon as he may.

His thoughts turned, once again, to his tent, and once again he pushed the idea away. To be deprived, forever, of that space... it was the only home he'd had, in so many long years. As long as he preserved that final fold in the cloth, his last visit there still lay ahead of him.

And there was no saying but that, someday, he might discover the means to renew its mysterious magics. Not, however, if he used the last vestiges up, and turned the miraculous bundle into naught but a scrap of cloth.

So, then, forward. 'Stout heart, ladies,' he said to the camels, and went to retrieve them. He would have to seek help at one or another of the two palaces, and given the choice, of course he must prefer the sunlit one. About it there hung an aura of peace and gentleness, light and hope, which could not but appeal to him, and thither he went.

But just as his right foot, swinging forth with purposeful stride, was on the point of crossing the divide into the sunlit realm, some barrier sprung up, a hazy, half-transparent construct which faintly crackled. When Baradir's foot encountered it — and then, propelled by irresistible momentum, his face did also — he received a slight shock, and was thrown backwards.

He lay for a moment, half stunned, as rain poured into his bruised face and soaked through his clothes. A great shiver revived him, the kind that shook him from head to toe until his teeth rattled. More accustomed was he to arid heat and sun; this creeping cold and chill rain were anathema to him.

Doggedly, he got to his knees, and then to his feet, and approached the divide once more. This time, it was with caution that he pushed one foot towards the sun, inching his toes towards that tantalising line between misery and hope.

For a heart-stopping moment he thought caution must succeed where confidence had not, and he might cross without interference. But, no. The barrier flashed back into view, and though it did have the courtesy to refrain from repelling Baradir by such force as before, he nonetheless found it impenetrable.

Some minutes he wasted in useless straining against it, with all the force (physical and sorcerous) that he could muster. It might only be an enchantment, yes, but the thing was as solid as stone. Baradir made no more progress trying to force himself through than he might by trying to shove his way into somebody's house, by way of the rear wall.

'Fasee,' he hissed. Throughout his ignominious endeavours, his three camels, curse them, had wandered nonchalantly over the warm sand beyond, backs largely turned towards their master in heartless unconcern. 'Fasee!' he shouted.

Fasee's head came up, and she looked long at Baradir, her left ear twitching.

'Fasee, come to me.' If a man could not cross the divide, perhaps a beast could? And though he could not convey himself into the blistering heat for which he so much longed, he might perhaps reclaim his companions, and the vital supplies they carried.

Fasee, bless her loyal heart, ambled in his direction — and halted as her nose collided with the barrier. She gave Baradir a look of shocked affront, took three steps back again, and wandered away back to her sisters, leaving him to his fate.

'Oh, very well,' sighed Baradir, accepting his predicament with what he hoped could be termed resignation. He turned his back on his faithless camel companions and marched away in the direction of the white-and-black onyx palace. The wind came in great gusts, tearing at his clothes, and a deluge of rain stung his eyes. Something unnatural howled behind the wind, an eerie keening which might, had Baradir been the cringing type of fellow, caused him to lose heart.

He set his jaw against these distractions, kept his face turned towards the beckoning black spire, and marched on.

It did not seem, after some minutes of effort, that he was gaining upon it at all. Stride though he might, the tower grew no larger, as though with every step he took he was somehow covering the same two feet of ground, and going nowhere.

He stopped for a moment to catch his breath, and mop uselessly at his streaming face. Then, again, he set off; and again, failed to draw any nearer to the absurd tower. With what apparent menace it loomed there, a dark fist raised to the skies, determined with its height and its gleaming black onyx to cause a flutter of apprehension in those who approached it! Its very unreachability was of a piece with such crude tactics, and if Baradir had had the managing of it—

A *whoosh* interrupted this happy flow of thought, and a sensation of rapid movement. Baradir, in fact, sailed through the space he had so utterly failed to traverse, and at such speed he could not, for some moments, breathe. He was then brought — for this had not occurred by his own efforts — to a sharp stop, his nose a bare three inches from the polished-black stone wall of the spire.

He gritted his teeth, and swallowed down a shout of rage. He had *no* love for the lands of the jinni, not when it meant being pushed and thrown about with so little consideration—

A line of light raced over the wall, tracing the outline of an arched doorway. This impromptu door fell inwards with a *crash;* stone-dust flew up, clinging to Baradir's skin and clothes; and a haunting voice from inside called, 'Come in, sorcerer.'

The power in that voice echoed off the walls, and reverberated through the floor. It shook Baradir's bones, raised the hairs on the back of his neck, set his heart to pounding.

Swallowing a sudden stab of fear, he strode through the door.

The moment he was fully over the threshold, the fallen stone vanished from beneath his feet. When he glanced back, the wall was once again smooth and unbroken behind him. All trace of the door had vanished.

7

THE HALL INTO WHICH Baradir stepped lacked distinguishing features, save for the uniformity of its black, polished onyx-stone. No windows lit the walls, and no furniture adorned the stark, echoing space within. All that met Baradir's eye was a spiralling stair set into the centre of the wide room, leading to somewhere above.

Baradir paused at the foot of those stairs, and gazed upwards. Something with the substance of storm-clouds obscured his view; no rain fell, to his gratitude, but to look up at that moment was to stare into the very heart of a vicious storm. The dark, roiling maw of it gazed back at Baradir, ablaze, now and then, with scattered sparks and searing bolts of lightning.

Baradir had the sense to look away.

He sought for some other means of progressing either forward, or back the way he had come, but nothing met his eye. He was sealed into the room with those stairs, and up the stairs he must go.

He set a foot to the bottom-most step, and began to climb.

The storm did not in the smallest degree lessen as he forced himself up into its swirling winds. The cloud, if anything, thickened, drenching him afresh with ice-cold dew, and sparks cascaded in showers over his clothes and hair; if he had not been so water-logged, he must have been set alight. The winds tore at him with great *shrieks*, howling again with those eerie tones he had first heard from a far greater distance. He set his teeth, trudged doggedly upwards on hands and knees, clinging to each step. Three times he was almost torn free of the stairs, and dashed to the ground below. Three times he hung on, flattening himself against the steps, refusing with a mixture of sheer strength and grim stubbornness to be swept away.

The climb seemed to him interminable, every second an hour — until, in the space of a single breath, it was over. He emerged onto a gallery far above the ground, where the winds did not blow, and no storm sought to tear him to pieces. Glancing down from this new vantage, he beheld a changed vision below: clouds there were still, but from this side they were pure white, and as gentle as could be.

All that remained of the storm was an occasional, thin, distant gust, whistling forlornly at the edge of hearing.

'Come in, sorcerer,' said that voice again, and its owner must now be much nearer, for he heard layers of tone in those words: a ripple of danger, the warmth of a desert wind, and a soft, dulcet purr... or was it a growl? She could have spoken from only feet away, but when Baradir, startled, turned about in search of the speaker, he saw no one.

Only another arched doorway, through which a strong light beckoned.

Motivated, perhaps, by the softness in that voice — or perhaps by mere vanity alone — Baradir wasted a moment's thought upon his clothes, and his hair. The briefest survey convinced him of the futility of all efforts to right the disorder in which he stood; his cloak hung heavy around him with all the elegance of a sopping dish-cloth, pouring a ceaseless trickle of water all over the floor. His hair was plastered to his head, his beard bristled with rain. He raked his fingers through both, abandoned the endeavour, and passed through the door.

'Yasmine,' he said, and stopped dead.

The infernal woman lounged at her ease upon a low divan-couch at the far end of the room. And what a perfect room for a lady to hold court, he thought bitterly, for it was a light, airy space, its walls and ceiling all glass, some of the panes daubed with colour, others clear all through. Outside her absurd palace all might be darkness and storm, but inside, somehow, she bathed in the soft radiance of a gentle, serene sunshine. Unlike the hallway downstairs, Yasmine's tower room was filled with furniture and paraphernalia, to the point of being cluttered. She had not gone to the Starlight Bazaars solely in search of him, he surmised, for fully half the contents of the room positively dripped sorcery, and could have come from nowhere else.

She herself was draped in sunset-coloured silks, with gauzy veils covering her hair. A dish of peaches in rose-wine sat upon a small, glass-wrought table at her elbow — Baradir's nose detected the tell-tale aromas even from some few feet away — and next to it stood the same, ensorcelled drinking-glass from which she'd been sipping the last time he had seen her.

She did not trouble to rise when he entered the room, but lay there, regarding him with an infuriating half-smile upon her painted lips.

'What is the meaning of this?' he said, controlling himself with an effort. He wanted greatly to stalk straight out of the spire again, but the thought of retracing his steps down those abominable stairs and stepping back out into the rain could not encourage him. And what would he do once he was out in the storm?

Yasmine sat up, reached out to her crystal dish, and selected a glistening chunk of peach-fruit. 'How have you been enjoying the feeling of powerlessness?' she said mildly, and conveyed the peach to her mouth, licking rose-wine syrup from her fingers.

'I do not believe anybody enjoys that feeling, lady.'

'Oh, you might be surprised.' She smiled. 'Some enjoy it very much indeed.'

'I am not of their number, which I imagine you very well know. Has all this torment been of your doing?'

Yasmine paused in thought, selecting another peach. 'That is a point worthy of debate,' she decided. 'Has it all been my doing, or your own?'

Baradir's fists clenched. 'If you imply that I have somehow revelled in self-torment—'

'Revelled, oh, no,' she interrupted. 'There would be no fun in that at all, would there?'

'I am intended to suffer, I collect.'

'Everyone suffers, Ibn Samar.'

'Do not address me by that name.'

'As you wish.' She consumed a third succulent peach, contriving, by her evident enjoyment of it, to alert Baradir to the emptiness of his own stomach. He had not had occasion to think of anything so ordinary as hunger or thirst in some time.

Well, he was thinking of those things now. And he was, as she had cruelly pointed out, powerless to alter even that simple state of want.

Curses upon her.

Yasmine, perhaps, saw this on him, and while she was not above drawing out the moment, she did at last relent. 'Shall you dine with me?'

'I would first know how I came here. How have you so manipulated me?'

'Does it matter greatly, to know the *how* of it? The fact remains that you are here.'

Baradir achieved a faint smile. 'Call it a matter of academic interest.'

'Oh! Then, it was the simplest of all things. I only let it be known, that should a gentleman of your description come asking about a certain palace of ensorcelled glass, he must be delivered at once to me.'

'How obedient, the jinni.'

'I did, of course, offer a reward.' She smiled at him, though the smile did not fully reach her eyes, and rose from her couch, casting the shimmering length of her head-scarf over her shoulder. 'We shall dine,' she decided, bidding him follow. 'And then, Baradir bin Samar, we shall talk.'

Baradir, powerless indeed, could only trail after her.

Yasmine led him out of her sunlit, glass-walled chamber, but to Baradir's further surprise, the room beyond was no longer the hallway through which he had passed, with its staircase leading down. Instead, the minaret's mistress entered an elegant dining-parlour, the informal kind, with a trio of silk-clad divans circling a low table of ebon-wood and white pearls. The table bore a heavy load of ornate silver-and-gold dishes, each piled high with succulent treats; Baradir's nose detected the savoury scents of roasted fowl, of rose-wine and mint, of honey and cinnamon and coriander. His gaze lingered upon a platter heaped with fried loaves, next to it a dish of syrup-drenched pastries, and beyond that a plate of savoury, herbed fish...

'You must be hungry,' said Yasmine, observing his preoccupation with a tolerant eye. She arranged herself upon one of the divans, its jade-green silks well-chosen to offset her sunset-coloured gauzes, and waved Baradir to take his choice of seat.

'My clothes...' Baradir began, but no sooner had he spoken than the rain drenching his garments began, in a rush, to evaporate; a rush of steam engulfed him, and when it dissipated, he was once again dry from head to toe. More than that, his previously crumpled sirwal might have been freshly laundered and pressed, and his cobalt-coloured mantle hung from his shoulders in a smooth, pristine flow of cloth.

Ah, the power of the jinni. Ever had it been seductive...

A growl of his stomach opportunely diverted his thoughts, and he seated himself upon a pearl-pale divan, attacking the nearest dish with alacrity. Spiced lamb, with apricots soaked in honey. He ate greedily, watching Yasmine with a wary eye the while, for still she had not answered his question. Nor did she eat; she reclined for a time, apparently oblivious to her guest, her gaze fixed upon a bowl of brightly-coloured sweets waiting near at hand; or, perhaps, upon nothing corporeal. She was deep in thought.

'I am the daughter of a jinn,' she said at last, without looking at Baradir. 'My son, Riad, is the progeny of another jinn. He is more jinn than man, but human enough for all that. He...' she paused, and her mouth twisted in bitterness. 'He has all the best and worst characteristics of man — and the best and worst of the jinni, as well. Even as a child, he was — headstrong. Ambitious. More powerful than I could understand, and yet he was not satisfied.'

'A common story,' Baradir acknowledged.

'Common enough, I grant you,' she conceded. 'But Riad is different.'

'How?' said Baradir bluntly, when she ceased to speak.

'He is... exceptionally powerful.' She shifted upon her divan, a gesture of discomfort — though whether of the physical sort, or a product of the turmoil in her mind, Baradir could not have said. 'He is a grown man, now, though still so young. He could equal your ancient power, Ibn Samar. Exceed it, if he chose. And I fear he does choose it. He—' she looked, briefly, at Baradir. 'He acquired his first jinn servant in only his seventeenth year. Six jinni now labour under his command.'

Baradir nearly choked upon a mouthful of stuffed aubergine. '*Six* jinni?' His mind reeled at the prospect of such power — not only that which six willing jinni servants would bestow, but the arts, whatever they were, that had secured six such loyalties to begin with.

Two or three more, and this slip of a boy, this Riad, would surpass his own achievements.

'I do not know what he is about,' Yasmine said, her face darkening. 'One would think he sought general dominion, but it does not appear to be that. Whatever it is, it is bound up with *your* palace. That is where I believe he has taken his jinni. And now they are all gone together.'

Baradir set down his plate, his appetite gone. 'My palace,' he said, and sat up. 'Is it here? In the jinn-lands?'

'I have sometimes heard reports of it in these parts. It is never there when I have endeavoured to catch up with it.'

His tent, then, may not have erred, in sending him into the lands of the jinni. Perhaps, at that moment, his palace *had* been somewhere nearby — though whether it remained so was another question.

Baradir knew not what to say, his thoughts in too much turmoil for clarity. He stared sightlessly at Yasmine, only peripherally aware of the gaze she directed at him. When at last he focused upon her face, he saw something there he was in no way prepared to combat.

Hope.

What cruel trick of fate was this? That *he*, Ibn Samar, notorious for his ambition and his cruelty and his coldness, should so many years later be this woman's only hope?

'Yasmine,' he said. 'I am not the man I was back then. I have told you I am no longer Ibn Samar, and it was the truth.'

'I know,' she said calmly. 'Upon *that* alone I depend. For Ibn Samar would never have had heart enough to help me. But, perhaps, Baradir bin Samar does.'

Baradir could have laughed — or wept. For his *heart*, of which she spoke with such confidence, was colder now than ever it had been before. Chill and brittle and cool, all sorcery now; not a scrap of humanity was left.

And he had given up hope that it would ever be otherwise again.

'I cannot help you,' said he.

For the first time, Yasmine bint Izebadd's composure cracked. He saw a glimmer of desperation in her dark eyes, a spasm about her mouth that spoke of a wearing tension, of unshed tears. 'Baradir,' she said softly. 'I *beg* you.'

'I cannot help you,' he said again. 'You must not hope for it. Have I not myself searched fruitlessly for my lost palace? It will not answer *my* call now, any more than it will answer yours. But...' he swallowed, for what was he proposing to *do*? And said recklessly, 'But I will try.'

A great breath left Yasmine all in the rush of a long sigh, and her shoulders sagged in relief. 'Thank you,' she said.

Baradir received the impression of a great, proud will humbled before him, and was surprised afresh. For *once*, the experience would have elated him. He would have revelled in his victory over this woman, daughter of a jinn as she was, and a power in her own right.

Now, he felt... discomfited.

'Do not thank me,' he said coldly. 'I will very likely fail you.'

8

'Your camels,' echoed Yasmine, some half an hour later, when Baradir stood tall and stubborn in the doorway of her sumptuous dining-chamber, refusing to be swept away. 'You will not leave without your *camels*?'

'They are my loyal companions,' said Baradir, for the second time. 'I will not leave them in these lands.' He had been about to say *treacherous lands*, and remembered at the last instant that these realms were probably her home.

He was prepared to encounter irritation in her, but instead she appeared... curious. 'More camels may always be got,' she observed.

'But these are *my* camels,' he said gently.

'Ah? And they have, I suppose, all your worldly goods loaded upon them.'

'There is also that.' Baradir thought of his tent, and wished again that he had kept it somewhere about his person, instead of in his camels' packs.

'I see,' said Yasmine. 'I need hardly tell you, I suppose, that if we succeed you shall have worldly goods beyond your wildest dreams? I shall not be ungenerous.'

The prospect of a full renewal of his tent's unique powers flitted across Baradir's mind, and was as quickly dismissed. That was for later. 'These are of personal significance to me,' he said, with as much patience as he could muster. 'As are my camels.'

'Well—'

'Lady,' said Baradir coldly. 'For a woman of your powers, this errand cannot take more than a few minutes to complete. Why do you object?'

He thought he detected dismay in her steady gaze. 'Just where are they?' she said. 'Why did not you bring them to my tower?'

'They are on the other side,' he said, and gestured generally in the direction he meant. 'Near the other tower.'

Definitely dismay. She gave a soft sigh. 'How came it that *they* came to be on the one side, and you on the other?'

'Ill luck.'

'Ah.'

She was silent.

Unease stirred within. 'They *can* be retrieved, can they not?' said Baradir.

'Of course,' said Yasmine crisply. But she'd hesitated.

'Then let us go.' Baradir turned to the door, and then stopped, remembering that he was in the presence of a jinn. If she had half her father's powers, she could deliver both of them to the sunlit side of the strange barrier in seconds.

'It is only that—' said Yasmine.

Baradir waited.

'That is my— my son's tower.'

'Ah?'

'It is an odd place,' she said, twisting her fingers together in a gesture of... restlessness. Nervousness? The play of arcane light around those slim brown hands proved distracting; Baradir half-closed his left eye, and the roiling colours ebbed. 'It is unstable. Riad made of it a place of... surprises. One never knows what will come of a sojourn in that realm, and nothing ever happens the same way twice.'

Baradir said, 'Hence the barrier. Your work?'

'Yes.'

'I will go alone,' he decided. 'If you will be so kind as to grant me passage beyond the barrier, I shall shortly return with my camels.'

She raised one brow, perhaps at the arrogance inherent in his words, but she made no objection. 'I see you cannot be dissuaded.'

'I cannot.'

'And, perhaps, it is well. For my son's agile mind will place tricks and traps aplenty before you, once we reach your palace. You shall have opportunity to grow accustomed to his ways.'

Baradir's lips curved in a faint, twisted smile. 'You do not know the half of it.'

She blinked. 'I don't?'

'My *palace*, you see, has hidden itself from me for a century. It will do its best to... inconvenience me further, should I manage to enter it, by every means at its disposal.'

'Your palace,' she repeated slowly, 'dislikes you?'

'Extremely.' This was not the truth; his palace possessed no mind of its own with which to form *likes* or *dislikes* in that fashion. But the idea was close enough to the truth, and Baradir need not pursue the point.

'It is a building,' said she, not unreasonably sceptical.

'A most unusual one.'

She swallowed. 'Perhaps its displeasure may have... softened, over time.'

'It is as inflexible in its opinions as I am.'

Her head tilted at that, and the look she gave him was pure speculation. But she made no further comment on the subject. 'Are you ready?'

'Perfectly.'

She said nothing further, only gave a negligent wave of one glimmering hand, and in so doing tossed Baradir away like a pebble.

He fell — feet-first, thankfully — into warm sand, a radiant gold under an improbably balmy sun, and for a blissful moment experienced a sense of perfect well-being. The odd little realm was serenity itself. *Broken,* Yasmine had said. *Unstable.* He saw no sign of it.

His camels, to his relief, did not appear to have come to any harm. Fasee and Talee were tucked up together in rest, twin mounds of thick fur and drowsing contentment. Hanee ambled about a few feet away, lips moving restlessly over the bare sands in a futile attempt at foraging. And that, thought Baradir, was a point of interest about Riad's realm: its eerie perfection. Not so much as a single rock interrupted the undulating sweep of pale gold that made up the heat-baked desert.

And, then, the clouds themselves were out of place. Here was a land without rain; without even the capacity for rain, he would judge.

The golden sand glittered.

Enlightenment came. Baradir dropped to his knees in the desert, and felt with both hands. The sand was faintly warm, rather less so than it ought to have been, and had an odd, brittle texture about it…

Powdered gold. The sand had naught to do with rock or earth or dust; it was pure gold, every fleck of it.

'So, then,' said Baradir to Hanee, who drifted nearer with every lazy step. 'The master here likes riches, hm?'

Well, but who did not? Jinni and human were alike in their unconquerable desire for all things precious and rare.

Still, perhaps it would be something he could use. Later.

He collected Hanee, towed her gently over to where her sisters lay asleep, and risked a few minutes spent searching for his stock of preserved apricots and dates. Hanee lipped at his sleeves the while, and tried to eat his hair; 'Yes, yes,' he told her, with affectionate impatience. 'I cannot move fast enough for your appetite, I know, but— ah, here they are.' His hair and clothes were preserved by the simple means of an alternative bribe; Hanee retired, satisfied, and Talee and Fasee did not object to an abrupt waking when they discovered such treats awaiting them.

Pleased by the contentment of his camels, and intent upon their needs, Baradir was slow to notice a gradual changing of the light. By incremental degrees, the bedazzling sunshine faded into a wan, greyish glow, and shadows crept in. When at last he glanced up, he was in time to note the swelling of great, airy clouds across the firmament: still dreamy and white, these, but darkening by the minute. Something ominous roiled somewhere deep within.

'Quickly, now,' he said, chivvying the camels along, and made haste for the barrier. It occurred to him, too late, that Yasmine had given no specific instructions for his passing back through it, and into the relative safety of her lands; he could only hope that she had arranged for its vanishment, at least for as long as it took him to hustle his charges over the invisible line.

In the event, he did not make it that far.

For, as he strode over the fiercely glittering sands in the direction of Yasmine's realm — so different was it, now, in his altered perception, that the very darkness of it struck him as a relief, compared to the brittle, changeful light of its neighbour! — he stepped out with confidence, his left foot encountered nothing, and down he went, his camels' lead-ropes falling from his hands as he fell.

He fell for some time, long enough to anticipate a painful, perhaps fatal, landing.

Instead, he drifted softly down into warm currents of air, his weight supported by some invisible force, and landed without injury in a darkened, lamp-lit space.

Or, no; the force ought ordinarily to have been invisible, were Baradir an ordinary man. But his left eye detected the agent of his preservation (if preservation it was): a formless being of swirling breezes, twin lights like bright, cunning eyes flashing somewhere within.

'Thank you,' he told the wind-spirit. 'And my greetings and obedience to your mother.' He had learned his lesson when it came to the little spirits (as Iskandar had called them); if the fairy of the winds chanced to be paying attention, he would not by any oversight wish to insult either her or her offspring.

Winds coiled around him, tugging at his clothes. He smelled something heady and floral, and then something bitter and sharp. The taste of cinnamon lingered, unaccountably, in his mouth.

He paused for some moments, awaiting further interference; for had the wind-spirit sought to spare him the consequences of so sharp a fall, or was it here as his jailer?

It did nothing more, however, only amused itself sailing about the place, stirring up the sands underfoot and causing them to dance to unheard musics; Baradir, slightly, relaxed.

And looked about himself. He was of a certainty in some manner of cave, and far below ground. A tilt of his head brought nothing into view but a ceiling of uninterrupted rock; whatever tunnel or channel he had fallen down was gone.

He was sealed in.

Baradir took a quick, deep breath, inwardly cursing fate in general, and collected himself. Little of any particular interest met his cursory inspection of the cave: it was not spacious, nor was it possessed of much in the way of contents. Golden lamps set into the walls cast a dim glow over dull, smooth rock and a sandy floor, and that was all.

He did, however, detect a way forward, for the lamps marched on into the near distance, beckoning him onward.

Bereft of alternatives, Baradir followed the lights.

He had not gone more than a few steps when something changed. The lamp-lights, hitherto clear and dim, flared up as he passed; colours blossomed in the floor, and in the rock walls; they were flowers, he saw in wonder, each wrought exquisitely from vivid coloured glass, though they unfurled delicate petals just as though they were real blossoms.

Why they should do so for *his* sake, he could not determine, and despite the beauty of the display it could not comfort or encourage him. The word *trap* floated through his thoughts, spoken in Yasmine's voice; and how better to trap a sorcerer than with a display of riches *and* magic, and of a particular sort to please him, at that? For he had worked many similar enchantments, back in the days at Mount Marikalat.

He proceeded with caution, wishing that he dared summon his own ancient arts. He had worked too much sorcery already, of late.

Perhaps you might, his heart said. *This is not your palace. You are no longer Ibn Samar.*

Cautiously, he mustered a wisp of his will; in response, a trio of frangipani flowers burst into a blazing glow: crimson, copper and lemon, the hues washed over their fragile petals and then faded to nothing.

Or, not quite nothing. As he passed, a faint, residual glitter of colour caught his eye; he turned his head, and saw a trail of glassy frangipani blossoming in the wake of his steps.

His lips twisted in a grimace. Attractive, doubtless. Useful in the face of some nameless threat? By no means.

He did not, as yet, dare risk more.

A twist in the passage guided him around to the right — and there he stopped, for his impromptu lamp-lit journey had come to an end. Ahead of him spread a wide, high-ceilinged cave, the walls of which were covered in a rampant array of glass and gems. They had formed twining, flowering vines and clambered up; they'd fashioned themselves into tumbling bouquets and spilled back down again; they'd crept inexorably across the floor, their progress halted only by a deep channel of water which snaked its way across the centre of the cave.

Baradir, dazzled, shut his eyes, and then cautiously opened the right one. Even with his mundane sight, the bejewelled array threatened to mesmerise; when he, carefully, opened up his left eye again, the colours intensified, shimmering with a deep, ancient sorcery.

Baradir's heart beat quick at the sight.

He *recognised* this.

In the centre of the cavern rose a great tree, of no species familiar to Baradir. Either it was a real, natural tree, or its glassy structure of gems and magic was so perfect as to give the illusion of it. True, dark bark clad the wide trunk, and the boughs stretching over Baradir's head had the haphazard, knotted structure of genuine, living wood.

Be that as it may, an enchanted tree it doubtless was; for besides the fact of its flourishing growth here deep underground, where no natural light could penetrate, there was also the curious nature of its leaves and fruits.

Baradir padded softly forward until he stood directly under those branches. The glassy vines underfoot were smooth and cool; he felt their chill even through the leather of his shoes. He reached up, and touched the tip of one finger to a single, delicate leaf. That, too, was cool, and smooth. It had no colour, this, but sparkled with a scintillating clarity that could only belong to the diamond-jewel.

All the leaves were like that. A cluster of berries that hung near Baradir's ear proved to be pure rubies, and another yellow sapphire; Baradir walked on, scrutinising leaf and fruit and nut in turn, and found them all of a like composition: jewels and glass, deeply ensorcelled, and in his troublesome left eye he saw the sorcery that had wrought them pulsing at the core of each ethereal jewel, like a heart.

When he stole, it was with the considered movements of a rational man, not the greedy grubbing of a street thief. He selected his acquisitions carefully: a trio of leaves here, a modest cluster of berries there, until he had filled two pockets with ensorcelled jewels. His prize piece was not a gem at all, but glass: mere trumpery compared to sapphires and rubies, *some* might say, but Baradir knew better. Ancient jewels knew themselves too well to accept any deep interference. Glass, though, was fluid. Glass could be moulded, coaxed into forms fresh and new, given a life and a purpose to suit the sorcerer. It did not object, the way diamonds did.

At least, not often.

Baradir's glass trinket was neither leaf nor berry but a beetle, plucked tenderly from a dazzling leaf and secreted inside a pouch all its own. A vivid thing, its carapace displayed two bejewelled hues: emerald-green until halfway down, and the rest azure-blue. Its wings twitched at Baradir's touch, but it did not otherwise stir, and lay afterwards quiescent in its hideaway.

Baradir, satisfied, took some further moments to absorb the sights before him; for when might he ever again witness such a spectacle? He had *heard* of trees that grew gems of perfect lustre, but never expected to encounter such a marvel.

What a pity he could not put the tree into his pocket, too, and walk away with it. Once his palace was restored to him, he would build the most perfect courtyard within which to house this wonder...

Regretfully, he turned away at last, and faced the shadowed mouth of the passage through which he had come. Then did it occur to him that he had not, in all his time down in the depths of the sands, discerned any hint of a possible exit. If he had imagined that the tunnel itself must at some point carry him upwards, and out again, he was now disappointed, for the jewel-cave was sealed. There was nowhere to go, but back.

Back, then; but to where? Back past the solemn rows of hazy lamplight, and into the dark? He had been as much trapped there as he was in this cave.

Well, then. *Needs must,* he told himself.

He reached out again, with his *other* self; the Baradir who had built one of the greatest wonders of his age; the Baradir he had so long suppressed. *Ibn Samar,* Yasmine would have termed him.

It was not the diamonds or the emeralds which answered him, but the humble glass. Fluid as water, and obliging, those glassy vines stretched themselves, unfurled their coiling tendrils, and raced in a whirling flurry across the floor, scattering rubies and amethysts in their wake. Alight with the glow of Baradir's sorcery, they wove and wound and wormed their way into a new configuration: a narrow, straight path leading right through the centre of the cave, and underneath the serene boughs of the jewel-tree.

Baradir drew himself up. 'When I pass down this path,' he said, and with every word a deep hum resonated through the floor, 'you will carry me farther than I can walk without aid. When I reach the end of this path, you will take me elsewhere, *out* of this cave.'

A low mist rose, a shadowed haze visible only in Baradir's left eye. There lay the magics that would smooth his passage out of this sealed tomb; he had only to walk along the path.

Baradir hesitated.

He had not specified where he would like to go, because he did not precisely know.

No; certainly he did. He must go back to the jinn-lands, and Riad's realm. His camels waited there, and Yasmine in her tower. And he had promised.

'You will take me—' he began, but got no further, for a gust of wind blew up from somewhere, and got hold of his ankles. His feet moved; he took three rapid steps, great long ones that gobbled up the ground, and within moments he had almost reached the end of the narrow path.

The wind-fairy's child. Gracious, why must it *now* interfere? 'No!' cried Baradir, and tried, too late, to halt himself. 'I pray you, permit me to pass out of here as I choose!'

The airy spirit, heedless, gathered itself up, and expelled all its air in so mighty a gust that Baradir was helpless before it. He had not time to appeal to the glass-wrought vines underfoot, so obliging as they had proved; he was swept along and away, and found himself, abruptly, elsewhere.

Ibn Samar? whispered a voice Baradir did not know. *Is that you?*

9

Baradir experienced the feeling of waking up, though he did not remember having parted with his consciousness.

Shortly afterwards, revising this idea, he instead developed the certainty that he was asleep after all, lost in the depths of a dream. For were these not the sumptuous walls of his own palace, rising around him?

How could that be, save that he dreamed?

He lay prone, in the centre of the room he had once thought of as The Chamber of Moon and Pearls. Every inch of it was glass, stained and frosted; the hues were the serene silver-white of moonglow, and the soft iridescence of sea-pearls.

Thus far it was familiar enough. But, the images formed among the glass were not what he remembered. A brutal storm tossed the ocean waters dominating one wall; the seas moved as he watched, roiling with anger and sending up bouts of sea-spray. The moon that shone down upon this unpromising scene was not so much tranquil as cold; a winter's moon, harsh and unforgiving.

The tides-in-glass flowed from wall to wall, washing the chamber in the ceaseless motions of a restless ocean, and Baradir felt the deep, dark cold of it seep into his bones through the floor.

The worst part, from his undignified recumbent position, was the ceiling. He received the clearest view of the rumbling storm-clouds depicted up there in glass; these, too, moved, billowing and thundering, with flashes of lightning racing diamond-white through the frosted panes.

Baradir felt chill droplets rain down upon his face, though when he put up his fingers to wipe away the rainwater, he found that his skin was dry.

'Hello?' called Baradir, suddenly mindful of the voice he had heard. Did he imagine the sensation of being under surveillance?

Nothing answered him. Slowly, he came to his feet, wincing at the pull of his chilled muscles; he may not *look* over a century old, but the curse that so hatefully preserved him had not been so kind about how he *felt*. He drew himself up as best he could, straightening his aching shoulders, and tried to resemble the dauntless, fearsome sorcerer he had once been.

Movement, everywhere, distracting his thoughts and shattering his focus; he could not think, not with such a water-dance going on all around him.

On a stray impulse, he shut his left eye. Instantly, all motion in the glass ceased, congealing into a frozen tableau of tumult.

'Hm,' said Baradir.

Still, no sound reached his ears save those he made himself. He might be alone indeed, save for the lingering feeling that *something* watched him.

He took a few, experimental steps in the direction of the grand archway beckoning at one end of the room. Through it, a clear light filtered, warmer in character than the cold light in this room. Baradir, desperate for warmth, could not help being drawn that way.

Nothing rose up to stop him, and the voice — or its owner — still did not emerge. Gaining confidence, Baradir walked on. If he was not mistaken, and this *was* his own palace, then beyond that door should be a corridor of sun-baked sands and golden light, all awash with desert roses. Walking down it, he would feel the warmth of that sun on his skin, smell the fragrance of the flowers, feel the sand shift and crunch under his shoes.

Something tugged at his heart, in remembering. This had been a place of such perfect wonder, once. He had made sure of it. Well, and if it was broken now, whose hand had wrought that disaster but his? If he would take credit for its beauties, he must take responsibility for its cruelties.

He was not very much surprised, upon reaching the archway, to find it melting away before him, taking the promise of light and heat away with it. Where there had been a portal, a solid wall now stood.

'Very well,' he said. 'If we must negotiate? I had rather expected such.' Daringly, he reached out a hand and laid it, palm-flat, against the wall where the door had been.

At once he felt suffused with a smouldering rage, so intense it stole his breath. Pulsing through his bones, emanating from the very walls of his beloved house, was a burning desire to *hurt* something. His palm smoked where it met the wall; he snatched his hand away and staggered back, appalled.

Distantly, he remembered. Had not those been *his* feelings, during his latter days as Ibn Samar? The palace... his poor, sensitive creation, so bound up with its creator as it had been. Always, it had responded to his wishes, his feelings, his desires, reflecting every shade of his moods.

Its very sensitivity had once been the source of its wonders. Baradir had dreamed up new chambers with a thought; altered the arrangement of old ones; created ponds and fountains and living jewel-trees as easily as he drew breath. He could walk at his leisure through the halls of his palace and his home would adapt itself to his wishes; if he were tired, there would be the perfect chair. If he were hungry, there would be a feast of his favourite delicacies. If he were tired, a comfortable divan or a bed.

Never had he dreamed that this adaptability would one day be the means of breaking it apart.

He stood for a while in silence, nursing his still-smoking hand, and regarded those wayward walls in resentful silence. 'We could have borne anything, you and I,' he told them. 'What was the disapproval of others, to us? We were unstoppable.'

A faint rumble in the floor was all he had for answer. Nonetheless, he understood it well enough.

He *had* been unstoppable. That had been the problem.

And it was not the disapproval of others that had done the mischief; it was his own—

To whom do you speak? whispered a voice, and Baradir started.

'No one,' he instantly answered, and felt a fool, for if he addressed no one then he declared himself the sort of eccentric who held conversations with inanimate walls.

It cannot hear you, you know, continued the voice, and it was the same one Baradir had heard in his last moments in the wondrous cave. *Not in the way that you think.*

'I know that very well,' Baradir answered coldly. 'And I ought, considering that this is *my* palace.'

Silence followed, for so long Baradir began to imagine himself alone again.

But then:

So you are *Ibn Samar,* the voice breathed, and a faint stirring of the air around Baradir's face alerted him to a definite presence in the room. Whatever it was, though, he could not detect it, not even with the water-fairy's touch upon his ensorcelled eye.

'Once I was,' Baradir corrected. 'I am not now.' He stood tall under the scrutiny of the faceless entity, in no way cowed, for this was *his* ground.

Once a sorcerer, always a sorcerer. The voice gave a distant chuckle; the flow of air over Baradir's face had gone, and he thought the words now emanated from the north-west corner of the room.

He strolled back into the centre of the storm-hall, and stood waiting. 'I rarely practice the arts, now. Tell me,' he added, deciding it time to go on the attack. 'Who are *you*, that you have taken up residence, uninvited, in another man's home?'

I, too, am a sorcerer.

'That I had reason enough to guess,' said Baradir dryly.

This palace alone is worthy of my power.

'I am to be flattered, I take it.'

It is I who is flattered, countered the voice. *That the great Ibn Samar should condescend to visit.*

'Not altogether voluntarily,' Baradir pointed out, feeling a flicker of unease, for the voice had developed a nasty, purring quality which spoke of some ill-feeling.

'You are Riad,' said Baradir, hoping to disarm his interlocutor.

He succeeded, for the faint breeze swirling about the room abruptly coalesced into a solid, human form, standing a scant six feet away from Baradir.

No, not human; not quite. For while the torso and arms and legs were those of a human male, this creature's feet were clawed paws, his hands sported long talons, and his head was that of a copper-furred wolf. He was far taller than he had a right to be, towering some four feet over Baradir's own, not insignificant height. He was big of frame, too, with great bulky shoulders and heavily muscled limbs.

A boy's fancy, thought Baradir, and refused to permit himself to feel intimidated — even as the jinn-wolf approached, with a predator's slow prowl, and stopped directly before him.

'How,' said the jinn, in a wolfish growl, 'do you come to know my name?'

'I have been in conversation with your mother.'

Riad answered only with silence.

'She is concerned,' Baradir persevered. 'For you, and for the jinni serving you.' He paused, attempting to gauge Riad's frame of mind, but the wolf's head defeated all efforts to read the boy. 'What is it that you want?' he continued. 'Do these jinni serve you willingly, as your mother believes? Or have you enslaved them?'

The snarling grew louder as Baradir spoke, and Riad appeared to lose all power of human speech. How he managed to force any comprehensible syllables out of that maw was beyond Baradir's understanding.

'What shall you do with such power, Riad?' Baradir persevered. 'Is it dominion that you want? Riches? Fame?'

'Enslaved,' Riad echoed at length, in a tone of contempt, and spat something else Baradir could not decipher. His copper-furred hackles rose high, bristling with a palpable rage.

Baradir silently attributed some of his palace's current mood not to himself, but to Riad.

'You are wrong,' said Riad, at length calming enough to speak. 'I have enslaved no one, and I do not seek any of the things you name.'

'Am I indeed wrong?' said Baradir. 'I have yet seen nothing to convince me of it.'

The low chuckle came again, but it was a nasty, mirthless sound. 'You have always been wrong, Ibn Samar. About everything.'

'Tell me truths, then.'

'A truth?' Riad's muzzle split in a wolfish grin — and then, to Baradir's discomfort, his bulky figure faded to nothing and disappeared. All that was left, once again, was that voice. *One of the jinni in residence here is my own grandfather,* the voice whispered. *If you imagine I would enslave my own flesh and blood, Ibn Samar, then you judge me by your own standards — not mine.*

'Izebadd?' Baradir repeated. '*Izebadd* is st-- here?' He had almost slipped, and uttered the word *still,* but checked himself.

The very same, said the voice, and the ghost of a chuckle came again. *As you well know. And you dare to suggest that* I *have enslaved him? I?*

'If he is concealed somewhere here—' Baradir began.

How could I conceal anything from Ibn Samar, in his own house?

The final words faded away into the faintest whisper. After this Riad spoke no more; Baradir was left in a heavy, oppressive silence, feeling obscurely discomfited.

The encounter had not gone at all as he had expected. Where was the brash, combative boy of Yasmine's description? And was he right, about Izebadd?

He was aware of a feeling of... disappointment. A century he had waited for this reunion. Now he stood at last in his own halls, but instead of making a triumphant return as long-lost incumbent, he felt an intruder.

If he had secretly hoped that the palace would welcome his eventual return...

He sighed, and sought to bring some order to his scattered thoughts. Never mind the conflicting tales and competing demands of Yasmine and her puzzling son; what did *he*, Baradir bin Samar, want?

Why, he wanted what he had always wanted. He wanted his palace back. And whatever their motives in crossing Baradir's path, either Yasmine or Riad had been the means — directly or indirectly — of placing him inside its beloved walls.

Well, then.

'If you are still here, Izebadd,' he whispered to the empty air. 'I had better find you.'

PART TWO: FASEE

1

Peacefully ambling after her master, her mouth full of succulent, chewy apricot, Fasee was somewhat taken aback when the sand opened up, and swallowed the man called Baradir in one gulp.

She planted her sturdy feet in the changeful sands and waited for the ground to throw him back up again. But when every trace of her juicy mouthful was, regretfully, swallowed, the sand still lay smooth and undisturbed before her, and Baradir had not come back.

Hanee was worried. She drifted nearer to Talee and huddled close, for though Tal was not the eldest, she had always been the calmest of the three.

Talee, true to form, flicked an ear and stood unmoved.

'Do you think he is coming back?' said Fasee at length, when perhaps half an hour had passed by.

'Yes,' said Talee.

'No,' said Hanee.

'When?' said Fasee.

Talee, uninterested, lay down. 'By the time I wake up, perhaps.'

With which words she shut her eyes.

Fasee exchanged a look with Hanee.

'What should we do?' said Han.

'Wait,' said Fasee with a sigh, and cast a suspicious eye over the rain driving down not twelve inches from her nose — a rain she could neither feel nor hear. Where *she* stood, the air was warm and dry, but some quality within it set her fur a-bristle. 'Perhaps we should—' she began, but Hanee interrupted.

'Someone is coming.'

Someone *was* coming, a thing shaped like a woman, though she moved like a thundercloud and wore stars in her hair. *Not* a woman at all, then, really. She strode through the darkling rain, and not a drop of it touched her.

She did not step into the sunny sands, but stopped a foot or two away, and regarded Fasee and her sisters with arms folded. 'What, then, are you?' she said.

The camels said nothing. Things shaped like men or women never did hear.

'Speak,' commanded the woman impatiently.

So Fasee tried. 'We are camels,' she said.

'Not on the inside,' said the thing shaped like a woman, and Fasee blinked in surprise. 'What are you, when you are not camels?'

'We are always camels,' said Fasee.

'You must have been something else, once,' said the woman.

Talee, waking, said: 'We do not remember it.'

The woman-thing stood, arms still folded, gazing upon the three sisters as though they had in some fashion displeased her.

But it was not they who had done so. 'Where is your master?' said the woman-thing next.

'Gone through the sand,' said Fasee.

A look of alarm crossed the woman-thing's face, and then her eyes turned curiously distant. For some time she did not speak.

Then, at last, she shook her head. 'He is no longer in the jinn-lands. All trace of him is gone. You do not know, I suppose, where it is he went?'

'Into the sand,' repeated Fasee.

'He will return,' said Talee, and added fatalistically, 'He always does.'

But the woman frowned. 'I am not sure of it. I do not know if even Ibn Samar—' She stopped speaking, leaving Fasee to drown, briefly, in the sea of her own confused memories, for those words had been spoken more than once of late. *Ibn Samar.* Why did they strike such familiar tones in her mind?

What did they mean?

The woman spoke again, and the thought faded. 'It is my fault that he has left you,' she said. 'And here you shall forever remain, if I do not extract you.'

'It is not so terrible, here,' offered Talee.

'But,' said Fasee, 'we have no food.'

'And no water, either,' added Hanee. 'The jinn is right, we cannot remain here forever.'

Fasee, surprised, took a fresh look at the woman-thing, and found that her sister was right. She was more woman than jinn to look at, but more jinn than woman within.

'Do you enjoy being camels?' said the woman-jinn abruptly.

Three camel faces looked blankly back. 'I do not know what you mean,' said Fasee with dignity.

'I mean, should you not prefer to be restored to whatever else it is that you are?'

Fasee shifted uneasily. 'But Baradir—'

'Ah yes, Baradir. How long have you been trailing about in the sands after him?'

'A long while,' said Talee.

'Not so very long,' corrected Hanee.

The woman-jinn looked at Fasee, who twitched an ear, and thought. 'We do not reckon the time so well,' she at last owned. 'It has been long, but not so long.'

The jinn-woman looked briefly at the sky, and drew in a slow breath. 'It is apparent to me,' she said slowly, 'that there is more to this than I can at present understand. How did you come to be teamed with Baradir? Did he purchase you? Was it *he* who bestowed upon you your present shapes?'

'It was not he,' said Fasee firmly, misliking what bordered upon an aspersion against Baradir. 'He bought us at market.'

'We made sure of it,' added Talee.

The jinn-woman's brows rose. 'Oh? Why?'

'We wanted him,' said Talee.

'We knew him,' added Fasee, praying that the curious woman would not ask too many more questions, for how could she explain further? They none of them knew how or why they recognised Baradir; only that they did, and that in doing so they had felt a strong compulsion to remain near him. For how long had it been since they had encountered anything familiar?

The woman regarded all three with a severe eye, but to Fasee's relief appeared to abandon the questions. 'I am Yasmine,' she said, and waited.

Fasee gave her name first, with a promptitude borne of relief. Her sisters were a little slower to follow suit, but soon enough Yasmine was making them a formal greeting, and — more to Fasee's alarm — approaching nearer.

'Do not startle,' said Yasmine. 'I mean you no harm. On the contrary, I shall do you a great deal of good. I cannot restore your original shapes without knowing what they were; but this information may be discovered, and the means found to change you. If you will permit me?' She stopped on the edge of the strange divide between sun and rain, and waited.

Fasee thought of her life as she remembered it: of long toils through hot, dusty climates, the weight of Baradir's trade-goods slowing her steps and her mouth caked with sand and grime.

She thought also of the piercing sweetness of the dates Baradir so often gave her, and the ecstasy of a long, deep, cool drink after many days without.

Of Baradir's gentle fingers stroking her ears, and of his voice crooning reassurances after a long and tiring day.

'I will permit it,' she decided.

'Then so shall I,' said Hanee, with more doubt.

Talee signified her concurrence with a dip of her proud head, and Yasmine nodded.

'We will have to be quick,' she said. 'I shall cause this barrier to vanish, in this space, and you will come straight through it to me. Is that agreed?'

It was too late for doubt; and what alternative was there, anyway? Fasee signalled her readiness, and when, moments later, a ripple in the air announced the absence of the barrier, she ran through, full-tilt, into the soaking rain beyond.

Whatever sorcery protected Yasmine from the rain did not extend to her. She was drenched in seconds.

'Well, then,' said Yasmine, permitting the sorcerous barrier to regain its place with a *snap*. 'Whose aid shall we seek? Someone who sees past the surface of things, perhaps.' She paused in thought. 'Or those with knowledge of things past.'

The camels had nothing to suggest.

'Tell me,' said Yasmine thoughtfully. 'Has *anyone* ever seen the truth of you?'

'No,' said Fasee.

'Not even Baradir?'

Hanee gave a snort. 'He thinks us camels through and through, and cannot hear us.'

'He has his own troubles,' said Fasee quickly.

Yasmine developed a look of acute interest. 'And what are they?'

But Fasee would say no more.

'It is his heart,' said Talee.

'What of it?' said Yasmine. 'Is he in some way ill?'

'No,' said Talee. 'Not ill, but cu—'

'*Hush,*' interrupted Fasee, shoving her sister with her nose. 'That is the master's business. He would not thank us for sharing it.'

Talee fell silent.

'Very well,' said Yasmine, and gathered up their three lead-ropes. 'But I will ask you again, by and by.'

'Why?' said Fasee, more in curiosity than resentment. 'What is it to you?'

'There is some great mystery about that palace,' said Yasmine, incomprehensibly to Fasee. 'It is all bound up with Baradir; it *must* be. And since it has captured my wayward son's fancy as well, the matter is of some importance to me.'

Since none of this made any particular sense to Fasee, she did not trouble to enquire.

Yasmine regarded Fasee for some moments in silence, though her eyes had gone distant again. 'It is the arts of the Xingqing I want to employ,' she mused. 'They *must* know of a way to uncover your past, and then much may be done. They may also have a means of finding what has become of your master, no? But it is so cursed difficult to find any of them.' She lapsed into thoughtful silence.

'We were there, once,' offered Fasee.

Yasmine looked sharply at her, alert. 'There? Where?'

'Xingqing Kingdom.'

'How?' breathed Yasmine, her eyes going very big. 'You were actually *in* the Kingdom of the Xingqing? Surely you cannot mean that.'

'We were,' said Talee. 'Master did not want to leave, but we had to.'

'He got blankets,' added Fasee.

'How?' said Yasmine again. 'How did you contrive to find it, let alone to enter it?'

'The tent,' said Talee. 'It's in my pack.' She turned herself as she spoke, offering her left side, and the pack slung upon it, to Yasmine.

Yasmine eyed the pack in question with obvious interest, but she did not move. 'Have I your permission to search?' she said. 'It cannot seem right without Baradir here. But, we are engaged upon business of yours, which is also business of his; and surely he cannot mind it?'

'He won't mind,' said Fasee cheerfully. 'There is nothing in it that's important, except the tent.'

So Yasmine approached Talee, and unfastened the carry-packs, and searched through them. 'I do not find a tent,' she reported.

'Oh,' said Fasee. 'That's because it looks like a bundle of cloth.'

'This?' said Yasmine, and drew out a folded length of fabric in many colours.

'Yes,' said Fasee. 'To use it, the master always shakes it out and then it becomes a tent.'

Yasmine, obedient to instruction, shook out the folds in the cloth — and, like always, the fabric swelled and billowed and twisted in the air, and when its gyrations were over a splendid, luxurious tent stood upon the rain-drenched earth. This time, it had gaily fluttering pennants.

'Now we go in,' said Fasee, and trundled through the entryway. Beyond, the tent was just as they had left it: Baradir's marvellous blankets lay folded neatly to one side of its silken quilted floor, and all the light was stained in the vivid colours of the tent's cloth walls. 'And when we come out, we will not be in the rain-lands anymore but instead—'

'Oh, but,' said Talee, 'we do not always go to the same place, when we leave.'

'It will not be Xingqing,' said Hanee, following Fasee into the tent. 'It was Xingqing only once, and the master said we could never have such luck again.'

Yasmine, by this time, stood in the centre of the tent, the roof of which soared over even her tall head, and looked around in some wonder. 'Is not this itself a Xingqing creation?' she suggested. 'I can think of no other likely source for such a marvel.'

'We do not know,' said Fasee.

'Do I understand correctly,' she went on, 'that the tent always goes somewhere different, when you emerge?'

'Yes,' said Fasee. 'Baradir sometimes tries to tell it where to go, but it doesn't listen well.'

'So its choice of destination is random?'

Fasee bobbed her head, her nose questing for any leftover fruits among the fat cushions.

'No,' corrected Hanee. 'Master once said there must be some structure to it, but he could not determine what it was.'

'It would then appear random,' agreed Yasmine. 'But perhaps it may be encouraged to return to its place of origin. I would stake anything I own on that's being somewhere among the Xingqing.' The tent's entrance glided closed behind Hanee; Yasmine crossed to it and tried to peep out again, but the silks would not yet part for her. 'Has your master ever tried that?'

'I don't remember,' said Fasee, and becoming aware of a growing tiredness, she lowered herself into a plump stack of cushions with a grateful sigh. 'I will sleep now.' Her eyes drifted shut. 'Wake me when we get to the Kingdom.'

'But—' said Yasmine.

Fasee heard no more. A delicious lassitude enveloped her, and she was asleep.

2

Fasee woke to a cold wind blowing about her ears, and a strong, sharp aroma filling her nostrils. She sneezed, twice, and got up all in a rush, shaking herself. Spotting Talee a few feet away, she ambled over and huddled close to her sister's warmth. 'No one said it would be *cold* in the Kingdom,' she complained.

Yasmine's voice answered her, though the jinn-woman was nowhere in sight. 'It is because we are up very high, I think.'

Fasee ventured as far as the tent's entrance, and poked out her nose. The flap had opened upon an indigo sky, hazy with moonlight and silver-touched clouds. Nothing else could she discern amongst the darkness.

She gave a sniff, and the sharp scent engulfed her. Was it... herbs? 'Is this the Kingdom?' she said, suspicious.

'I am not yet sure,' said Yasmine, her voice definitely coming from beyond the walls of the tent. She was outside, in the cold. Fasee did not much want to join her, but she did want to see the fabled Kingdom. Pausing to grasp Baradir's marvellous blankets in her teeth, she passed out of the tent, Talee drifting along at her heels.

Yasmine stood a few feet away, with Hanee. Fasee waved the blankets at her, but so absorbed was Yasmine in scrutiny of their frigid surroundings that she paid no heed.

Fasee, shivering, stamped a foot.

'Oh,' said Yasmine, and took the blanket. She draped its luscious folds over Fasee's broad back, and immediately a balmy warmth dispersed the chill. There was not much to be done about her feet, or her nose, and Fasee resigned herself to a little suffering.

'It is not *that* cold,' said Hanee with some scorn. 'No worse than the desert at such an hour.'

'I *hate* the desert at such an hour,' said Fasee.

Hanee snorted.

'Do you think it will be hot, when the sun rises?' added Fasee in hope.

'No, I do not,' said Hanee.

'Likely not,' echoed Yasmine. 'We are up high, as I said. A mountain-top, perhaps. Though, I would think the air would be thinner.' She took a deep, deep breath, as though to prove this point to her satisfaction. 'There are clouds,' she added, looking — to Fasee's confusion — down towards the ground, rather than up into the skies.

Fasee, detecting only a pale blur, wandered away some steps, and saw that Yasmine was right. The blur gradually resolved itself into a mass of wispy cloud, floating far nearer eye-level than it had any right to.

'A puzzle, is it not?' said Yasmine. 'For if we are up so high as to have reached the clouds, we ought not to be so comfortable.

There must be deep magics at work, and that encourages me to hope that we are indeed arrived at the Kingdom.'

'It is an empty Kingdom,' observed Fasee, for around her nothing stirred. As far as she could discern, the mountain-top upon which they stood (if it was a mountain-top) was empty apart from Baradir's tent.

Upon which thought, even the tent collapsed into a pool of cloth, leaving them without either company or shelter.

Yasmine, bending to collect the erstwhile tent, gave a low cry of dismay. 'But it is nothing but cloth now! How can that be?' She picked up the fabric, and shook it, and all it did was flap about listlessly, like any other length of cloth.

'Oh, dear,' said Fasee.

Yasmine looked hard at her. 'Fasee? Do you know what's happened?'

'Well, it's obvious. All the enchantment has gone out of it.'

'Yes, but why— no, never mind.' Yasmine sighed, and folded up the cloth. Even so arranged, it did not resemble the neat bundle Baradir had been used to use. It was only cloth.

Yasmine hid it in some tuck in her garments, and said: 'It is too late to worry about that now. We must—'

But a voice broke in, interrupting her. It was an old, dry, dusty voice, and it spoke, seemingly, from everywhere. 'Where,' it said, 'did you get a Twelvefold Pavilion?'

'Twelve folds!' said Yasmine. 'That must have been the twelfth fold, then. What wretches we are, to have used the last one.'

She did not seem perturbed by the bodiless voice, and so Fasee did not take exception to it either. 'It was master's,' she offered. 'Where did he get it, Han?'

'I don't know, and neither do you. He had it before he had us.'

'Oh. Then, we can't help you,' said Fasee.

The source of the disembodied voice now came into view, and Fasee observed that it was not bodiless at all. It had quite a solid body attached to it, in fact, once it had finished materialising; one of moderate height, and most likely of the male type, though this she judged more from the voice than any distinguishing feature, for the speaker was swathed from head to foot in silk. A great hat crowned his head, its brim so wide that it obscured more than half of his face. A jade-coloured scarf wrapped his throat, and spilling from his shoulders almost to the floor was a splendid robe of bright sky colour, trimmed in something green and shimmery. Covering every inch of these silks were painted symbols, which drifted dreamily across the surface of the fabric, swaying and coiling and uncoiling themselves in unwontedly lively fashion.

Fasee stared at this vision, mesmerised, and was further startled by a wisp of ruby-red smoke darting from beneath the brim of that outrageous hat. A goldish pipe, she now saw, emerged from somewhere within that scarf, its mouth lodged between the speaker's lips. Every time he paused in speech he took a puff; and the ensuing smoke, sometimes ruby and sometimes azure or amethyst or jade, escaped from his mouth — or, not always, for here came a stream of it pouring from the hem of the robe, and a stray wisp emerging from the cuff of one wide sleeve.

So absorbed was she by this collection of marvels that she had no attention to spare for the words he was exchanging with Yasmine. When she gathered herself enough to listen, she was in time to hear him say, in the accent of one speaking a tongue not his own:

'—mistaken, quite mistaken! We do not deplore "intruders"; visitors delight us. You doubt that it can be so?'

'You do not precisely encourage visits, do you?' answered Yasmine. 'Few can say they have ever found their way to your Kingdom.'

'Precisely, precisely,' said the smoker. 'Those, then, with the wit and — shall we say, the need? — to make the attempt, and what's more to succeed at it — well, what merchant could ask for a better customer?'

'Ah,' said Yasmine.

'You, doubtless, have arrived here with some pressing request you would like fulfilled.'

'As a matter of fact, I have.'

'Very good.' The enrobed man took a great breath, and waves of amber-coloured smoke erupted from hem and cuff and collar. This lot smelled spicy, like the cakes Baradir sometimes bought at the Bazaar, and had been known to share with Fasee. 'Shall we agree, then, that you are *my* customer? I have found you first, have I not? And a lady of such wit and exquisite manners could hardly be so rude as to purchase elsewhere.'

Yasmine looked the man over. 'Hm,' she said. 'Shall we agree that I shall not be so rude — provided you can supply me with precisely what I need?'

'That,' said the smoker, 'would be a fair bargain.' Upon which he bowed, sending a stream of smoke in Yasmine's direction.

'Excellent,' she said, wafting away the smoke with a wave of her hand.

He bowed again. 'You may call me Ru.'

Yasmine returned the greeting. 'You may call me Yasmine.'

'Do I mistake?' said Ru, some tilt to his great hat suggesting he examined Yasmine with close interest. 'I address one of the jinn peoples?'

'You have a keen eye.'

'Two of them,' agreed Ru. 'But one is a little keener than the other.'

'And what does your keener eye tell you of my companions?'

Ru looked about — turned all the way around, in fact, and ended facing Yasmine again, but without having so much as glanced at Fasee, or Hanee, or Talee. 'Your companions?' he repeated.

Yasmine pointed a finger at Fasee. 'Three of them,' she elaborated.

'Oh!' said Ru, and she had the doubtful pleasure of enjoying Ru's intense scrutiny herself. He spent some time over it, and it struck her that he looked in much the same way Baradir had lately looked, since the water-fairy; namely, that he detected *something* interesting about her, but could not decide what it was. 'Camels,' he said at length. 'And yet—'

'And yet, perhaps not,' said Yasmine. 'My first request pertains to them. I would know what they once were, that I might find a way to reverse whatever enchantment they are under.'

'Intriguing,' said Ru. 'I collect that there is another request?'

'One more. I would find the way to a great palace of ensorcelled glass, that once stood—'

'At the top of Mount Marikalat,' supplied Ru.

'You know it?'

'All know of it.' Ru puffed for a moment, and smoke billowed afresh. 'What would you with that place?'

'That is a personal matter.'

'Do you propose to enter it?'

'Yes.'

Ru lapsed into silent thought again. 'I believe I can supply both of these needs,' he said, when he had emerged from his thinkings.

'I am delighted,' said Yasmine. 'And what shall be your price?'

'My price,' echoed Ru. 'Ordinarily gold, lots of it; or perhaps some wonder of similar value to those which I bestow upon you. But in this case...'

'Yes?' prompted Yasmine.

'My *price*, is simply this: when you enter the palace of Ibn Samar, you will permit me to enter it with you.'

Yasmine, visibly surprised, did not speak for a moment. 'Why should you wish for that?' she said.

Ru, briefly, smiled. 'The Xingqing are famous, are we not?' he said irrelevantly. 'Our marvels of magic and wonder are beyond compare. There is no one alive who would not give an eye-tooth for the smallest and most insignificant of our treasures. Is it not so?'

'I know your works to be highly regarded among my people, certainly,' agreed Yasmine.

'See!' said Ru. 'Even the mighty jinn bow before our skill! But. There is a but, here, and its name is Ibn Samar.'

'Was,' said Yasmine, without thinking, for she looked conscious directly afterwards, and said no more.

'Well, perhaps he is dead,' allowed Ru. 'Perhaps he is not. There is no saying, with a man like that. You see, he is of great interest to *my* people, for being the only sorcerer of any stamp whose creations — *one* of them, at least — can be said to rival our own. Or whose fame, one might as well add, has come close to eclipsing our own.'

'You are jealous,' said Yasmine.

'No!' said Ru, plainly appalled. 'I am in *awe*.'

'What?'

'Prostrated with admiration,' continued Ru. 'I would see this wonder for myself. I want to study it. I want to understand how it came into existence; how it was made; how it functions. I want to *experience* it.'

'Is that all?' Yasmine's tone dripped suspicion.

Ru's tiny smile reappeared. 'Perhaps. Let us also say... if it should prove to be abandoned, in this age far beyond that of its creator, I may also wish to — ah, adopt it?'

'I believe you shall find that you are not alone in that notion,' said Yasmine.

'Possibly so, possibly so,' agreed Ru. 'For who could hear of such a palace, and not covet it?'

'Me, for one,' said Yasmine.

'And yet, it is your heart's wish to find it.'

'I have reasons,' she repeated. 'Never mind what they are.'

Ru bowed again. 'It is of no matter,' he decided. 'Let us begin with your delightful camels, yes?'

Fasee found herself the centre of both Ru's and Yasmine's attention again, and did her best not to shrink back under the combined weight of their scrutiny. 'Will it hurt?' she said.

'I don't know,' said Yasmine, with an honesty Fasee felt compelled to appreciate, even if it could not reassure. 'Are you willing?'

Fasee gave a sigh, and thought regretfully of calm, comfortable Baradir and his pockets of never-ending fruits. 'I suppose I am,' she said ungraciously.

Yasmine repeated the question to Hanee and Talee.

'*Yes,*' said Hanee, with an emphasis that surprised Fasee. 'Who would choose to be a camel, who had the power of being anything else at all? My back *hurts.*'

Yasmine bestowed upon her a brief, commiserating pat, and looked enquiringly at Talee.

'Yes,' said Talee simply. 'Though,' she added, 'I hope it will not hurt very much.'

'We will all hope for that,' said Yasmine. She looked, then, at Ru, and said: 'What arts, then, can you bring to bear upon these poor creatures?'

Ru looked from Hanee to Fasee to Talee, and for a while the smoke ceased altogether. 'We will go,' he at length announced, 'to my sister.'

'Oh?' said Yasmine.

'She is an enchanter of prodigious skill,' he explained. 'And she has a Seeing Pool.' He began to draw upon his pipe with great inhalations, sending out billows of smoke in many colours.

These streamed across the floor, mingling with the soft wisps of mist and cloud, and began to solidify. Before Fasee's amazed eyes, the smoke became a wide carpet of intricate design, its corners adorned with tufts of silk.

Ru stepped onto it. 'It is big enough, I think, for all three,' he said, and waited.

Yasmine took Fasee's lead-rope, and gently tugged her forward, until all four of her feet were squarely upon the carpet. It felt soft under her feet, and fluffy, and she could not at all understand what they were any of them doing upon it.

But when Hanee and Talee and Yasmine herself were all likewise assembled, the carpet gave a jerk and a shudder and began to rise into the air.

Alarmed, Fasee dropped at once into a crouch, her legs too much a-tremble to hold her. 'I want *Baradir*,' she sobbed, and hid her face in the carpet's soft pile.

She felt the fleeting pressure of Yasmine's hand upon her head, right between her ears. 'We'll find him soon,' she promised.

Fasee lay like a stone, and waited.

3

The carpet, lurching unsteadily with every gust of
wind, and repeatedly threatening (in Fasee's view) to throw
them all off again, swooped and climbed its way across unknown landscapes (unknown to Fasee, who stubbornly refused
to open her eyes, or to peep over the carpet's edge). When at last
it came to a stop, Fasee, urged on by Yasmine's gentle tug upon
her lead-rope, got to her feet. Her legs were as stout as noodles by
that time, and her stomach flip-flopped in queasy somersaults.

'Are we *stopped*?' she demanded of Yasmine.

'We are.'

'For good?'

'For now.'

Fasee eyed both Yasmine and the carpet suspiciously, but
since the one favoured her with a reassuring smile, and the
carpet had the decency to make no further movements (and
since her elder sisters had preceded her off the thing, and stood
with cool unconcern to one side), Fasee consented to force her
trembling legs forward, and exited the carpet.

Ru had gone ahead of them all. Looking down her long nose
in his wake, Fasee beheld a small village of perhaps eight or

ten houses, each one shaped like a stack of square boxes piled atop one another. The roofs of these dwellings were rather wider than the walls they sheltered, which reminded her of Ru's hat. Ornate gables and carved and painted window-frames and doors added a prettiness to the scene of which Fasee approved, or would have if she were not so intent upon the struggle to remain upright.

Water flowed everywhere. Narrow, clear channels of it ran in between each pair of houses, so every house had its own arched bridge, as handsomely decorated as the gables of the houses. The trickle and babble of slow-moving water soothed Fasee's spirits, and she quieted.

Ru being all but vanished into the distance, Talee and Hanee set off after him at an ambling pace, and Fasee brought up the rear with Yasmine.

Their destination proved to be a house, slightly bigger than the rest, rather taller, and situated a little apart from the others. Fasee caught a glimpse of some unidentifiable contraption crowning a balcony-space upon the roof, and had time only to think that Baradir might have approved of it, for she detected the sheen and the glitter of enchanted glass.

But Ru was going inside, and the door through which he entered the house was patently too small to admit Fasee or her sisters. 'Take them around to the back,' Ru told Yasmine as he disappeared.

At the back lay a garden of such enchanting beauty that Fasee forgot her misery at once. Tall, willowy trees with pale bark and red, frilly leaves ringed the space. The rest was filled in with a pattern of winding stone pathways criss-crossing their way in between aromatic shrubs, whose leaves Fasee longed to sample, and bright flowers in hues she had never before beheld.

'The Seeing Pool?' said Yasmine.

'What?' said Fasee, tearing her attention from the tantalising fragrance of a particularly succulent bush, just inches from her nose. 'Oh.' The garden, she vaguely discerned, made up a series of concentric circles marked out in shrubs or bushes or flowers (and eventually, trees). Marking the precise centre was a perfectly circular pool, and by the shimmering, dark-jade colour of its waters, Fasee judged it to be very deep indeed. Its surface was undisturbed by any weed or plant or insect, nor did the breeze seem to touch it. It waited there, silent and inert, and peculiarly inviting.

Ru emerged from the house, and with him came a second person, shorter, and clad in much more sober fashion than he. Her robes (for this must be the sister he'd spoken of) were a dull green colour, with no symbols on them at all, and she wore what looked to Fasee like a plain black scarf wrapped around her even blacker hair. She paused upon the threshold of her garden, and regarded Fasee and her sisters through dark, serene eyes which crinkled at the edges.

'I see,' she said, and bowed to Fasee.

Fasee dipped her head in response.

'And how long have you been this way?' she inquired.

'I don't know,' said Fasee.

The brows of sister-of-Ru went up at once. 'You have no memory of a different time?'

'None whatsoever,' said Hanee.

'Well,' said the lady, in a brisk tone. 'We shall soon have it cleared up.' She strode forward towards the Seeing Pool, and Fasee hastily scrambled out of her way. 'No,' she said, and gestured to Fasee. 'Come, come.'

Fasee obeyed, and soon found herself positioned on the very edge of the Pool. She felt an odd reluctance to look into the jade waters, as inviting as they were, and stood in awkward indecision.

Ru's sister gazed calmly at her. 'If you do not wish to know,' she said, 'You do not have to look.'

Fasee thought about that. Did she want to know? What if her real shape was something awful? What if her life before this one had been terrible?

'Well, *I* wish to know,' said Hanee, coming up on Fasee's other side. She lowered her nose almost to the water's surface, and stood silent, gazing.

Fasee waited for some reaction of her sister's, by which to gauge the venture's success. But Hanee stood as though mesmerised, and not so much as a muscle did she move.

When Talee followed suit, and stood likewise enthralled (but at least, unappalled), Fasee grew ashamed of herself, and ventured forward. Swallowing her nerves, she thrust her nose down towards the Pool, eyes tightly shut.

Taking a deep breath, she slowly opened them.

A camel's face stared back at her. Her own.

She waited, but nothing else happened, and she felt a rush of disappointment.

And puzzlement, for was it a perusal of their own faces that held her sisters so rapt? Surely not.

As she was about to withdraw, however (in mingled relief and disgust), an alteration occurred. Her camel's face faded away, and was replaced by a human one. A face she recognised.

What was Baradir doing in the water of the Seeing Pool? He looked younger than the Baradir Fasee knew. His face was largely unlined and less careworn, his hair and beard black and thick, without the threads of grey that had since crept in.

He looked... haunted, Fasee thought. Something shadowed his eyes, as though he bore many invisible burdens, and there was an angry quality about his clenched jaw.

Fasee, gazing, thought she knew this Baradir, too.

Then Baradir's face vanished, and Fasee saw two more things in quick succession: a fleeting glimpse of a palace of glass and jewels, shining under the serene light of a crescent moon and scattered stars; and then, another face.

This one she knew. No doubt about it.

'It's me,' she said in wonder.

A girl stared back at her from the water's depths. She was slight, and probably not very tall. Something almost fey in her little features, for she was not very old, this girl; perhaps she had lived only eleven years, or twelve. Her black hair erupted around her face in an unruly mane, unbrushed, though someone had tied a sapphire-coloured ribbon into it. Her black eyes were bright with mischief, and she appeared on the point of laughter.

'No,' said Fasee, changing her mind, for she did not recognise any part of her own character in this girl's visage.

Ru's sister said: 'She *was* you, once.'

Fasee, unable to tear her eyes from the girl's face, made no reply.

'She could be again,' pursued the enchantress. 'If—'

She was interrupted by a resounding *splash,* and a wave of the Seeing waters rose up and soaked Fasee.

'*Cold,*' gasped Fasee, and shook herself.

Hanee was gone.

'Han!' yelled Fasee.

'She fell in,' said Talee, unmoved.

'What?' Fasee set off on an anxious circuit of the Pool, whose surface had subsided once more into placid serenity. If Hanee had gone in, she had disappeared completely, and the waters showed Fasee only her own camel-face. 'Han!' she yelled.

'Wait,' said Talee.

'*Wait*? She'll drown!'

'Does *she* look worried to you?' Talee jabbed her nose in the direction of Ru's sister, and indeed Ru himself. The siblings stood on the edge of the pool, Ru's smoking proceeding with rhythmic calm, his sister standing with her hands folded at her waist and her eyes bent upon the Seeing Pool.

Neither, Fasee had to admit, appeared at all disturbed at the water's swallowing her sister. Neither did Yasmine; and Fasee thought, suddenly, of the way the sand had gulped down Baradir in the sunlit land beside the rain, and how unremarkable the jinn-woman had apparently found *that.*

She huffed out a sigh, wished bitterly that people would stop descending without warning into places from which they ought not to emerge unscathed, and tried to mimic her sister's immoveable calm.

She did this without much success, but her nerves were spared when a hand erupted suddenly from the surface of the Seeing

Pool: a slim, long-fingered, human hand, young and strong, and followed by a forearm.

Then a head, attached to which Fasee was quite ready to believe there must be a body, too.

In short, a young woman floated there at the centre of the Pool, drawing in huge gulps of air, hair as black as Baradir's plastered about her face and neck. 'Yes,' gasped the girl, in Hanee's voice. 'I like this *much* better.' Then she laughed.

'*Han.*' Fasee lunged forward, forgetting for one crucial moment that she could not walk upon the water, however unusual it was.

Down she went, with all the grace and promptitude of a boulder.

Unluckily, halfway down, she inhaled.

❧ ☙

Her own exit from the Seeing Pool proceeded along far less dignified lines than her sister's. She was hauled out by Ru and Yasmine and lay upon the hard stone, choking and coughing up gouts of jade water.

This process, of necessity, distracted her, and some fifteen seconds passed before she observed that the appendages upon which she supported herself were *hands,* real ones, with five fingers each, and arms, and everything. The wind-tossed hair she'd glimpsed in the Pool's reflection hung in sodden ropes around her neck, and even the realisation that she was stark naked hardly discomposed her at all. Every inch of her was *hu-*

man. Her furless skin gleamed, polished and black and perfect, in the light of Ru's sister's garden.

Combing those restored fingers uselessly through her tangled hair, Fasee wept.

'But, no,' she said, sitting up, her tears forgotten. 'I am not Fasee, I am Fasani, and you are Hanizani—' Here she threw herself upon her eldest sister and squeezed half the life out of her— 'And there is *Talandani*, oh Tal, do you remember now?'

'Yes,' said Talee-that-was, sixteen and human and unruffled, if a bit out of breath. She sat with her human-again legs still dangling in the waters of the Seeing Pool, looking wide-eyed at everything.

Fasani became aware of the joint gaze of Yasmine, Ru and his sister fixed upon her, or her sisters, and began at last to mind about their collective nakedness. She covered herself as best she could with hands and hair, and said plaintively, 'Now I shall be *always* cold.'

'You were always cold as a camel,' said Hanizani without sympathy.

Fasani, ignoring this, began an entreaty for some manner of clothing, but found that Ru had anticipated her request, for he was puffing up a veritable storm upon his odd system of pipes. The last time the smoke had streamed away from him like that, a carpet had been the result. This time, the emerald-hued smoke wreathed her slender form in a cloud so thick there was no seeing through it. When it dissipated, she wore a robe much like his, though hers was emerald-coloured like the smoke. The garment contained layers upon layers of fabric, she now discovered, for it was heavy — and warm.

She beamed her thanks to Ru — the more so when, sticking out one foot, she discovered it to be stoutly clad in leather.

'Now I am ready for anything,' she declared, bounding to her feet, all worries and woes forgotten.

Yasmine regarded her thoughtfully. 'How came you to be camels at all?' she said. 'And what did it have to do with Baradir — as, I suspect, it must?'

'He is our father,' said Talandani, emerging freshly-clad from a cloud of amber smoke.

'At least,' said Hanizani (garbed in indigo), 'so said our mothers.'

'They would not have lied,' said Fasani hotly.

'Likely not,' agreed Hanizani. 'But Baradir always denied it, so *one* of them was lying.'

'Or confused.'

Hanizani directed at Fasani the kindly look she had always detested — the one that said *you are a fool, little sister, but you're forgiven,* and said nothing.

'He didn't want us,' explained Fasani.

'To be truthful,' said Talandani, 'nobody did.'

'I think,' said Yasmine, 'if you don't mind, you had better explain.'

4

'It is not a long tale,' said Hanizani a little later, when all were assembled around a low, circular table in the enchantress's house. Each of the sisters bore a laden plate upon her knee, as did Yasmine. Fasani, faced with the first full, human meal she'd had opportunity to enjoy in a hundred years, declined to talk. Leaving the tale-telling to Hani, she cheerfully stuffed herself with steamed rice and soup.

'We come from a small kingdom very far away,' continued Hanizani. 'You would not have heard of it. Our grandfather-the-king had twelve daughters, and ours was a poor country, and growing poorer. So he sent them all away to seek their fortunes elsewhere. Two were sent to the sorcerer-court of the man known as Ibn Samar, for even we had heard of his power and wealth; and rumour had reached my grandfather's ears of a palace, just completed, and more splendid than any other upon the earth.'

Yasmine gave a soft sigh; a sound, Fasani thought, of disappointment.

'You may guess the rest,' said Hanizani with composure, and paused to consume a morsel of rice. 'Ibn Samar would not wed.

My mother left his court before very long, and Tala and I were born at grandfather's house.'

'My mother stayed,' Fasani volunteered, having almost cleared her plate. 'And stayed and stayed, for years.'

'Why?' said Yasmine.

'She loved him, she said.'

Hanizani said, 'But at length even she returned, bringing Fasani with her. She said he had changed too much; he was eaten up with arrogance, and obsessed with his accursed palace, and she'd have no more of it.'

'Anyway,' said Fasani. 'Ten years later, more than half of grandfather's daughters had come back, and some of them brought children as well, and grandfather said he'd have no more of that, either. So he sent us back.'

'To Baradir?' said Yasmine.

'To Ibn Samar,' corrected Hanizani. 'He did not become Baradir until later, I think.'

'Not the Baradir *we* know,' said Fasani, and put down her plate. A sole dumpling remained there, succulent and inviting, but she could not now eat it. Her stomach churned. In her mind, visions of Baradir as she'd known him — kind, dependable, loyal — warred with his alter ego, Ibn Samar, as her mother (and Hanizani's and Talandani's mother) had depicted him.

'Who is the Baradir you know?' said Yasmine, and she looked upon Fasani with a compassion that brought a lump to her throat.

'Not like *that*,' she managed.

'He is not arrogant, at least,' said Hanizani.

'More the opposite,' put in Talandani.

'He *ought* to condemn himself,' put in Yasmine, rather hotly, 'if he could be so cruel as to — as to turn you into beasts of burden!'

'Oh, no!' Fasani protested. 'It was not *him* that did that.'

'We don't think it was,' said Hanizani. 'He was not pleased to receive us, but he was not unkind. More... aloof. The palace, when we went there, was not the place our mothers had described. It was overflowing with people; half of them, we were convinced, were there for no good purpose. Ibn Samar spoke of them with resentment, and we could not understand why, if he did not want them there, he did not throw them out.'

'Most of them were sorcerers,' said Fasani. 'Or enchanters, or the like. They all wanted to know how he had created the palace, what he had done, how it worked. They begged him to teach them. And some of them threatened him, and said how he deserved to be destroyed for all the bad things he'd done.'

'None of them really *tried*, of course,' said Talandani with cool disdain. 'He was far too powerful for that.'

'I suppose he enjoyed being so,' said Yasmine, her face as forgiving as stone.

'He probably did, once,' said Hanizani fairly. 'That being what my mother was on about. But by then I thought he was more... tired, than anything else.'

'And angry,' said Talandani.

Hanizani inclined her head. 'One night, a few moons after our arrival, everything went... wrong. We woke to confusion, and shouting, and an earthquake, or that's what it felt like. The roof fell in, in our wing, and almost killed Tala, so we fled.'

'Everything was wrong,' said Fasani. 'There was fire some-where, and three people were crushed under falling walls, and—'

'They were the threatening ones,' put in Talandani. '*I* wasn't sorry. They were cruel to us, too.'

'Anyway,' said Fasani, 'by the time the dawn came, half of the palace had fallen down, the rest was a mess, and we were camels.'

'It wasn't just us,' put in Hanizani. 'Some of the other people were cursed, too. I saw one turn into an acacia tree, and two more went away as desert foxes, and a third—'

'Was Baradir cursed?' interrupted Yasmine, with an intent look Fasani welcomed in place of her earlier fury.

'Yes,' said Hanizani. 'But not in the same way. He *looked* the same, last time we saw him — he wasn't a tree or an animal or anything like that — but he seemed... different.'

'Broken,' said Talandani.

'But,' said Yasmine. 'All this was a hundred years ago.'

Hanizani shrugged. 'We have not got any older. Neither has Baradir. That was part of the curse, of course.'

'Oh!' said Fasani, straightening. 'Do you think now we might?'

'Get older?' said Talandani, visibly appalled by the prospect.

'Most likely,' said Hanizani. 'You'll grow up at last, Fas.'

⁂

Much more conversation followed, though as it largely repeated everything that had gone before, Fasani's attention wandered.

In fact, she slept, curled in a chair, as she had not done in so many years.

When she woke, she discovered herself to be wrapped in a blanket very like Baradir's — the one she had just lost, she realised with a swift stab of guilt. She had been wearing his blanket when she had gone into the Pool, and had not been when she got out. It must now be somewhere at the bottom of the water, if bottom it had.

Plus, the packs Han and Tal had been carrying were gone, too.

Seeing as they had lost every item of value Baradir had owned, she could not imagine he would be quite pleased to see them again.

Despite this, Yasmine seemed bent upon two points: the finding of the palace, and the finding of Baradir, if it shouldn't turn out that the two could be accomplished by the same means.

'He may, perhaps, already be there ahead of us,' Yasmine was saying as Fasani woke. 'His disappearance was unexpected, but we *had* just been discussing the matter, and he had agreed to help. He might have waited for *me,* then, and I wish he had, but if he is to be found in the palace I shan't have too much to say to him about it.'

Fasani sat up, shedding the blanket. 'If he is in the palace then we have to hurry,' she said. 'It's dangerous in there.'

Yasmine smiled at her. 'He is no weakling, Fasani.'

'I know that,' she said. 'But the palace destroyed him once before, didn't it? It could do it again.'

Yasmine looked thoughtful. 'Did it? Which of them destroyed the other, do you suppose?'

Fasani, about to make a sharp retort, stopped herself, for the question suddenly intrigued her. What *had* really happened, upon that long-ago night? Both palace and creator had come out of it broken, and despite having been present, she could not have said how any of it came about.

'Well, but anyway,' she said, dismissing this question in favour of more urgent concerns. 'How are we to find it?'

'We have just been forming a plan,' said Yasmine, indicating Ru and his sister with a wave of her hand. The trio sat with their heads together on the other side of the neat, comfortable room, upon three chairs of some light, pale wood, with cushions beneath them and cups of something in their hands. A cast-iron pot, steam escaping from beneath its lid, sat on a low table before them.

They had obviously been there for some time.

'I hope it's a good plan,' said Fasani. 'We don't have much time.'

'We go to Sulanah,' said Yasmine. 'It is where Baradir was born, you know, and there have been rumours of sightings there these past moons.'

'Of Baradir?'

'Of the palace.'

'I've never been to Sulanah,' Fasani announced, and went to find her sisters.

'There is more—' Yasmine began, but Fasani would not wait to hear it. Let Yasmine and the others make the plans; Fasani wanted only to carry them out, and as soon as possible.

5

Ru's CARPET SWEPT THEM away from the Xingqing Kingdom later that same day.

'Had we not better wait until morning?' Hanizani had objected, observing the sinking sun through the window with eyes full of misgiving.

'I think it would not help,' said Yasmine. 'The palace is only ever seen at night, remember, or so report would have it. And it will not take us long to reach Sulanah.'

Nor did it. Either the Xingqing lived much nearer Sulanah than seemed probable, or Ru's carpet was more marvellous even than it appeared. Howsoever it was, the journey there was completed at a rapid pace, and in a short time; in less than an hour, the monotonous desert over which they principally flew gave way to the lights and more varied topography of a city.

Fasani enjoyed the procedure much more than she had before. Camels were not made for flying, she concluded. Neither were humans, doubtless; but seated comfortably cross-legged atop the carpet's soft, giving surface, lighter in weight and far more agile, and with only two legs to worry about keeping in contact with the rug, she was able to watch over the side without suffering unduly from sickness. A sense of excitement stole over her, especially when the lights of Sulanah came into view, and she stared in wonder as they flew over the white-walled city, tucked into the embrace of a wide sea opening to the west.

A place of prosperity, she thought; nay, splendour, even, for she saw many large houses, gleaming in white, with minarets and tall walls and perfumed gardens surrounding them. In the centre of these, atop a tall slope, was a palace belonging, perhaps, to a sultan.

But the carpet did not stop in this salubrious area. If Baradir had indeed been born in Sulanah, he had not grown up in any of these handsome houses. The carpet soared onward, and bore them to a place of very different character. Situated near the edge of the city, not far from where the buildings gave way to the harsh landscape beyond, gaggles of huts huddled together, several of them half fallen down. This Sulanah seemed another city altogether, for the gardens were gone, and the walls, and the gilded minarets. To Fasani's secret dismay, Ru said: 'Somewhere here, I believe,' and the carpet began to descend.

When it stopped, she stepped off it into a curling street thick with dust and choking with a heat only just fading with the dusk. Several of the mean little dwellings here were ruined, their roofs fallen in and windows empty of life. The rest showed few signs of habitation, and none whatsoever of either prosperity or joy.

Fasani frowned. Could proud Ibn Samar really have begun his life *here*?

'Are you sure?' she demanded of Ru.

'Yes,' he said.

'How do you know? You have never met Baradir.'

'I have not,' he agreed. 'But for one, the world has many tales to tell of that one, and all the stories agree that Sulanah was his place of birth.'

'Yes, but it might not be *here*.' Fasani looked about with distaste. 'Maybe one of the nicer houses?'

Ru's next words sounded, for some reason, apologetic. 'You see, I have been making use of an advantage.'

'What advantage?'

'I do not know if anyone else has ever gone searching for the precise birthplace of Ibn Samar, but if they have I doubt they found it. They did not have you.'

'Me?'

'And your sisters. To discover a place of origin, you see, it is best to have the person whose origins you are tracing with you. That, or something very personal of theirs. And what could be more personal than a daughter?'

Fasani, remembering long-ago Ibn Samar's appalled denial of fatherhood, quietly put this thought away for later perusal. 'Well then,' she said. 'Which house is it?'

'No,' said Hanizani, stretching her long limbs. 'Why are we here at all, Ru? We were looking for the palace, not father's birth-house.'

'That, too, is to do with the personal,' said Ru. 'There is a deep bond, between an object and its creator. Never was that more true than between your Baradir and his house, I think.'

'That makes no sense,' said Hanizani.

'Why does the palace appear in Sulanah?' Ru persevered. 'We know that it has not been at its creator's direction. It has not been at anyone's direction, as far as we can discover. If it comes here, then I believe it does so because it has absorbed the idea from Ibn Samar. In short, it is connected to this city as much as he is.'

'And therefore, to the house he grew up in,' said Hanizani, in a voice of scepticism.

'Perhaps,' said Ru.

'Do you mean,' said Fasani, 'that it's looking for Baradir?'

Ru looked at her in silence. At least, she thought he did. Still she could not see his eyes, under the sheltering brim of his wide hat. 'That is an intriguing idea,' he said.

'But,' said Yasmine. 'By his own account, Baradir has been looking for the cursed building for many years, without finding it. If it is so desirous of finding him, how have the two not encountered one another long before now?'

'I wonder if Baradir knows where to look?' said Ru simply.

'Surely he must know the place far better than we can.'

'I am sure he did once,' said Ru.

'But it's broken now,' put in Fasani.

'Yes. Meanwhile, the Baradir of today is *not* the same man as the sorcerer of old. Have I not understood that correctly?'

'So it would seem,' Yasmine allowed.

'Baradir has moved beyond this place, but his creation has not. So, then, we search.' Ru declared the subject closed by setting off down the shabby street, his head turning this way and that as he examined each one of the dwellings he passed. How he expected to know at a glance which one was once Baradir's, Fasani could not guess. But neither did she comprehend how his smoke-carpet worked, or the blanket she'd lost. So she swallowed her questions and objections both, and with Hanizani and Talandani by her side, she followed him down the street.

Yasmine came behind.

He went all the way to the end without stopping. At this point, the street abruptly ended. No wall protected it from the scrubby land beyond, nor boundary marker declared the limits of the city; it simply stopped.

So did Ru.

'Hm,' he said, and turning swiftly about retraced his steps all the way back along the street, to its other end. There it emptied into a small square, with branching paths leading off it into the depths of the city beyond. Someone had set up a small stall there, and the smells of cooking emanated from it. Fasani's nose detected onions, cinnamon, and something meaty. A small crowd awaited whatever the finished product of the cook's endeavour might be.

Fasani beheld the stall with great interest, but Ru ignored it. 'It may be,' he said calmly, 'that the precise house in which your father was born is no longer standing.'

'That would be a problem,' said Yasmine.

Ru paused in thought. 'I think you must do it,' he said.

'Me?' said Fasani.

'And your sisters. With my help, of course. Are you willing?'

'Yes,' she said, without hesitation. Talandani said the same, and, after a moment, so did Hanizani.

'Good. Then, I am going to blindfold all of you.'

Fasani felt a moment's unease.

Seeing this, perhaps, on her face, Yasmine smiled at her. 'Don't fear. I shall be beside you.'

Fasani straightened her shoulders. 'Very well. And then?'

'Then I shall lend you my magic, for a few minutes. You three will walk along this street once more, and if I am right in my surmise then at some point you will stop.'

'And that's the bit where Baradir's house used to be?' said Fasani.

'I hope, yes.'

Ru tied lengths of silk over Hanizani's eyes, and Talandani's, and then finally over Fasani's. 'This is to avoid confusion,' he said as he worked. 'If you try to look with your eyes, you see, you may become distracted, or focus on the wrong things. I want the magic to work unimpeded.'

'We understand,' said Talandani. She set off first; Fasani heard the soft sounds of her leather shoes against the dusty stone street as she walked slowly forward, leaving the space to Fasani's left empty.

Next went Hanizani, and then Fasani herself. Yasmine, true to her word, remained close.

What became of Ru, she did not know.

But soon she lost all awareness of others, for without her sight to show her what really stood all around her — and with, she imagined, Ru's magic to encourage other senses — she began to experience the street very differently. She saw, in her mind's eye, another street, much like this one but less decrepit. Many of the houses were the same in character, even if they were newer, their roofs sound (enough). Some were different, in style and shape and everything, as though built by people of ideas quite separate from those that now held sway.

It was before one of these that Fasani stopped. A humble place, of only a single storey, with a plain wooden door and two square windows either side, it did not suggest that its occupants had possessed much in the way of material wealth. But its white walls were clean; its structure was sound; and placed to one side of the door was a collection of stout clay pots, in which succulent plants grew. A poor place, but respectable.

'Ah,' said Ru.

Fasani listened, but heard no further footsteps. Her sisters, then, had also stopped.

Then someone took away her blindfold.

'Oh,' she said in confusion.

She had travelled farther than she had realised. So had Tala and Hani. They had progressed beyond the end of the street, and stood some twenty feet away from the nearest building. Ragged scrub lay beneath her feet, and open sky above, and that was all.

'I admit I am disappointed,' said Ru, looking about. 'I had hoped to find some means of passage, between an old house of Ibn Samar's, and the one he built. But there is nothing here.'

'There is earth,' said Talandani.

Ru pushed back the brim of his hat, and for the first time Fasani saw his eyes. They were, to her great surprise, a bright, clear jade in colour; *so* pure, and so polished, they might not have been real eyes at all, but semblances carved from jade itself.

'Earth?' he said, looking at Tala, and then at everything else.

'Of course,' said Yasmine. 'Baradir vanished through the ground before, did he not? In the jinn-lands, when he left you.'

'He didn't mean to,' said Fasani quickly.

'Oh?'

Fasani, unable to explain, shrugged. 'He didn't look like he knew he was about to disappear. He just went. We were on our way back to you at the time.'

'I wish you had said that before,' said Yasmine, with something like chagrin. 'I had thought his passage deliberate—'

'Never mind,' interrupted Hanizani. 'If we can walk a similar route, we can find him for ourselves soon enough.'

'But, how?' said Ru, though he did not sound as though he truly meant to enquire of anyone. He more asked the question of himself. 'You do not, I suppose, know by what means he vanished?'

'No,' said Talandani. 'The sand opened up and down he went.'

'Sand,' repeated Ru. He looked up. 'And was it night time?'

'No, it was very sunny.'

'But,' said Yasmine, 'these were the jinn-lands, and specifically my son's realm. He has chosen that it should always be something like sunshine, there.'

'Something like?'

'He cannot really dispense with the night, any more than I can banish the sun in mine. It is only an illusion.'

'So it may have been night, somewhere behind the false sun.'

'Perhaps. It is impossible to say.'

But Ru did not seem to mind this vagueness. 'Sands and starlight,' he said to himself. Then he took a small, glass bottle from a tuck in his robe, one that resembled the bottle Baradir had bought not so long ago. This one had a jewel in the stopper, just like his, though Ru's ran along vivid green lines.

He opened the bottle, and something shot out.

'Hold a moment,' said Ru calmly.

Whatever it was, held. Fasani saw only a nebulous shape etched against the sky, like a spray of sand in an oncoming wind-storm.

'Will you help me?' said Ru. 'In exchange you shall have your liberty.'

No response came, at least that Fasani could hear, though the little spirit did not depart.

'Will you make sand of this earth beneath our feet?' continued Ru. He looked up once more, and Fasani did likewise. The firmament stretched, limitless, above, the last light of the day all but gone. Stars were winking into existence. 'You know the kind I mean,' Ru said, and Fasani hoped the spirit did, for she did not at all follow. 'We would go through it, to Elsewhere.'

The spirit hung motionless for some moments longer, and then vanished from view. Fasani's heart sank, for if the sand-spirit — or whatever it was — would not help them, what more was there to be done?

But then the earth rumbled under her feet, and lost its firmness. She sank three inches, and felt the give and crunch of parched sand beneath her.

'Thank you,' said Ru, with quiet satisfaction, even as he sank by two feet at once.

Fasani grabbed at Hanizani, for she was sinking faster. 'Are you sure this is a good idea—' she shrieked, and then the ground rose up to gulp her down, just as it had done with Baradir.

6

Fasani fell, screaming (to her later shame). She experienced the curious sensation of falling, not just down but backwards; and not just in space but also in time. Before her precipitate fall came to an end, a barrage of memories passed through her mind, at such speed she could not grasp them all. She glimpsed her sisters, her mother, Baradir; the home of her childhood, and the palace, and the Starlight Bazaar; a glance down at her own camel's feet, and the memory of a night wind over her ears.

She saw the palace as it had once been, before everything had gone wrong.

When at last all this befuddling motion ceased, Fasani was left prone upon some hard floor, her mind whirling with colour and confusion. She lay still for several moments, her eyes squeezed tightly shut, unwilling for the present to open them and find out where she was got to.

Nothing greeted her arrival, as yet, but silence; a deep, deathly absence of sound. So profound was this, she was startled by the soft noises of her own breathing.

'*Well*,' she said aloud. 'Are you going to lie there with your eyes shut all night, Fas?' She said this in the crisp tone she imagined Hanizani would use, and it worked. Her eyes popped open, and she sat up, and took a swift, breathless look around.

First point of interest: she was alone. Hanizani and Talandani and Yasmine and Ru were all gone, nor was there anyone else in sight.

As for *where* she had ended up; the familiarity of the room tugged at her heart. Huge and echoing, it was, so large as to dwarf little, slight Fasani, sitting alone in its centre with her arms wrapped tightly around her knees. It had always been odd, this room; she did not know what it looked like to anyone else, for it had always changed whenever she had walked into it. Long ago — a hundred years, she'd been told, though it did not seem half that long — this had been her favourite of all the many chambers in Ibn Samar's enchanted palace. When she had set foot over the threshold and stepped eagerly inside, the shifting, glassy walls in their infinite colours had rippled and wavered and shifted, dizzying and exhilarating. When the tumult settled, Fasani saw depicted whatever most pleased her, outlined in the vivid stained glass of the sorcerer's contrivance. She'd had her favourites among the visions it produced, and what now met her eager gaze was her very favourite of all.

The desert at night covered one, long wall, its sands shimmering in rich gold, and motes of scintillating diamond scattered across its indigo skies. The palace itself was a part of this mysterious scene, viewed as from a distance: glass walls, tall minarets, and the grand dome of its roof, all so familiar to Fasani. *This* was the first glimpse she had ever received of what was to become her new home (however briefly); she and her sisters had purposely awaited its descent from the heights of its mountain-top eyrie, and crossed the desert in the chill of the night to reach it.

As Fasani watched, the palace-in-glass wavered like a heat-mirage, and vanished in a mischievous flourish.

The opposite wall showed Fasani the perfect garden of her imaginings, improbably abundant with blossoms of such size, only enchantment could prevent them from tumbling off their stems, and being trodden underfoot. Great moths of unlikely size fluttered through the night-skies above, and Fasani could almost smell — no, she *could* smell — the heady fragrances of the midnight flowers.

And in the domed ceiling arching overhead, she saw into the waters of a clear lake, its bed an expanse of pale sand littered here-and-there with bright jewels. Fish in as many vibrant colours swam lazily about, some of them blowing dancing bubbles into the waters. Fasani found she had lain down again, and was content to remain prone, gazing up at the serene underwater kingdom arching above her.

Thus it was that she was taken by surprise, not long afterward.

'Oh,' said somebody, the sound sharp and loud in the silence, and then added something else, in a tongue Fasani did not know.

Fasani gasped, and sat up again. 'What?' she said. 'Who are you?'

A door in the far wall, hitherto shut, now stood open, and upon its threshold stood a stranger: a woman, clad in lengths of cotton the colour of cinnamon, and with (oddly) an amber-painted turban of pure silk wrapped around her head. Jewellery glittered and shone all about her person: heavy gold bracelets hung about her wrists, copper chains were draped around her neck, and great hoops dangled from her ears. Every article bore inset jewels: rubies, garnets, amber-stones and beryl, and more. Fasani detected the odd glimmer of sorcerous magic about them, like the gems Ibn Samar had been used to wear.

This woman, though, in no other wise resembled the old sorcerer. Promising crinkles lined her eyes, indicative (Fasani hoped) of a merry nature, and she looked not at Fasani but at the glass-glamoured room around them both, her eyes wide with just the kind of appreciative wonder Fasani herself felt.

'I said,' the woman continued, in Fasani's own tongue, 'it has never looked like this before.'

'Oh, but it has!' said Fasani.

'Forgive my impertinence,' said the stranger. 'But how did you achieve this effect?' She looked at Fasani at last, and smiled. 'I have been trying to coax the place to change itself, and have always failed.'

'Oh!' said Fasani, and got to her feet. 'Is it so very difficult?'

'For me, yes.'

'I don't know,' said Fasani. 'It has always done it for me.'

'You are a sorceress?' said the stranger, looking Fasani over with a scepticism Fasani found pardonable, under the circumstances. She did not resemble a sorceress.

'No,' Fasani admitted. 'I never had any magic.'

'Then how...?'

Fasani shrugged. 'It has always done it. I have only to come into this room, and it changes.'

'Always?' The stranger's eyes narrowed, perhaps, in suspicion. 'I am very sure I've never seen you before, and I've been here some time now. I took you for a recent arrival.'

'I am. I've been away.'

'You got *out*?' This piece of news struck the woman in some profound way, for she stared at Fasani as though unable to believe what she had just heard. '*How?*'

Fasani blinked. 'I— it was long ago.'

The woman gave a gesture. Light flared briefly at her wrists, and when it faded a chair had appeared; gold-wrought, like her bracelets, and laden with plump, red cushions. Into this article of furniture she slowly sank, and sat there looking flabbergasted. 'You see,' she said, 'no one *else* has managed it this long while. I certainly have not, and I cannot tell you how I've tried.'

Fasani considered this. 'You mean you've been trapped here alone for a hundred years?'

'A hundred—' repeated the woman in a faint voice, and shook herself.

'The walls were falling down,' said Fasani, rather apologetically. It hardly seemed fair that she and Hanizani and Talandani had escaped with such ease, if this woman had remained a prisoner. 'So you see, it was not at all difficult to escape.'

The beturbaned woman looked keenly at her. 'Collapsed walls? But there are no collapsed walls, and I *had* thought I had gone all over this place.' She tapped a finger against her chin in thought, and Fasani caught a flash of ruby colour. Even her fingernails were bejewelled. 'You will help me,' she decided, and appeared exhilarated. 'Could it be that there is some part I haven't seen? Yes! It is possible, for I cannot walk through walls, and if the doors are hidden — yes, yes. There is more, I quite see it now. And in *those* parts, perhaps, there is a way out. You will help me?' It was a question this time, and directed at Fasani with a look of mingled hope and desperation.

Of course, Fasani could not refuse such an entreaty. 'I will help,' she said. Honesty compelled her to add, 'If I can. It's been a long time since I was last here.'

The woman rose at once from her chair, which collapsed instantly into a puddle of smoky water, and evaporated. She made Fasani a bow of infinite respect. 'I am Sharan, and it is my honour to meet you.'

Fasani made her best courtesy back. 'I am Fasani, and the honour is mine.'

Sharan looked Fasani over in patent curiosity. Fasani could not wonder at her feelings, for she must make an unusual sight: young indeed to be (apparently) adrift in the world alone, her colouring and features a mix of the Mako people and Baradir's Zunaht heritage, yet clad in the fashions of the Xingqing...

Apparently choosing not to enquire, Sharan busied herself instead with unwinding the turban that covered her hair. The sorceress made an odd sight herself, Fasani reflected, bedecked in ensorcelled jewels as she was — and that turban, for never had Fasani seen a *woman* with such an accessory.

And Sharan seemed now determined upon removing it entirely. No simple process, this, for the turban appeared to contain far more cloth than had been apparent when it was wound up. Length after length of it came out, and when at last it was all unbound, revealing Sharan's thick white hair, it seemed enough to make three or four turbans, at least.

Sharan shook out the silk, and it billowed out in length after length, impossibly long. The silken surface did not long remain blank: black marks rose up and darted across the cloth, as though put there with strokes of a fine brush. Maps appeared, racing down the silk, as though Fasani flew at unthinkable speed over an ink-etched landscape.

At last, the silk ceased to ripple, and settled into quietude. There upon it lay the intricate outline of a great house — doubtless, the palace.

'This is the work of many years,' said Sharan with quiet pride, watching her magical map materialise. 'This is the room we are in.' She knelt before the folds of silk, and pointed one long, sapphire-set fingernail. A neat rectangle was drawn there, though as Sharan gestured, the map moved, displaying a vivid image of the very chamber in which they stood, bright with colour. To Fasani's fascination, the silk recreated the room exactly as it now appeared, even with her own dreams colouring the ceiling and the walls.

Sharan spoke rapidly, her hands darting here and there as she pointed out other parts of the palace. 'That room is where I first came in. It is not much; perhaps it was a store-room, once. Here is where Aravinda joined us, and Barakat, and this was Zaki's entrance. You are the only person who has appeared in this room; perhaps it means nothing, but then you are the only person who, having once got away from the place, has for some reason come *back*, so perhaps that has something to do with it. And—'

'Excuse me,' put in Fasani. 'But— do you mean to say there are three other people here, besides ourselves?'

'*Three*?' said Sharan, looking at Fasani in astonishment. 'Why, child, there are far more of us than that. At least fifty, though I am never sure I have met everyone. It's a tricky place.'

'Fifty,' said Fasani, and for some reason her stomach dropped in a feeling of mild dread. Why? Perhaps because the palace of marvels had been still more crowded with people, when all had gone wrong, and Fasani had long wondered whether that had been a coincidence. For the place had felt full of... bustle, and not the exhilarating, friendly kind one encountered at, say, the Bazaars. It had been a chaotic tumult, a mess of competing wants and ambitions and desires... there had been, always, conflict.

'Fifty,' said Fasani again, and frowned. 'All trapped?'

'I do not know of anyone who has got out again,' said Sharan. 'But then, you know, I wouldn't hear of it — afterwards. Would I? And I have not, as I said, necessarily met everyone.'

'How did you all come to be in here?'

Sharan's answer was a wry look. 'Much the same way *you* did, child, I would say.'

Or in other words, by strange sorcery under the stars, and with or without one's strict intention. 'We must get everyone out,' said Fasani.

'Child, do you not think we have all tried?'

'No,' said Fasani. 'You don't understand. The palace doesn't *like* people, you see.'

Sharan began to look as though she were unsure of Fasani's sanity. 'Doesn't like?' she echoed.

'No. Or perhaps it was Baradir who didn't like the people. I never could be sure which — or if they were different things at all. Maybe they weren't. If Baradir felt bad, then so did the palace.'

'Who is Baradir?' said Sharan, rather sharply.

'Oh,' said Fasani. 'He was Ibn Samar, then.'

Sharan's hand shot out and fastened around Fasani's wrist. Her grip did not precisely hurt, but her fingers squeezed too tightly. 'You were here in the time of *Ibn Samar*?' she said, breathless.

'I—' said Fasani, and stopped. She had been about to volunteer more of her identity than might be wise, and thought better of it. 'I was,' she said instead. 'It was a hundred years ago, or so they say. I don't remember it being so long.'

Sharan began to look a little wild. 'You cannot be more than twelve, surely.'

'I'm not,' Fasani agreed placidly.

'Then how—'

'Strange magic, and starlight,' said Fasani, with the smile her mother had once dubbed *mischief pure.*

Sharan released her wrist, and made her a brief bow of apology. 'Forgive me. Tensions run high in this place, you know.'

'Yes, they do.'

A swift look was her response, and narrowed eyes. 'Why did you come back?' she said, abruptly. 'Did you mean to?'

'I meant to. I'm looking for—' she stopped. 'Someone,' she ended lamely. Some instinct told her not to reveal that Ibn Samar still lived. She did not yet want to discover Sharan's reaction to *that* piece of news.

Sharan digested this in silence, and to Fasani's relief she did not enquire further. Instead she said, after a long pause: 'What was he like?'

'Who?'

'Ibn Samar.' Sharan breathed the words with a kind of awed reverence, mixed with a little... fear? Anger?

Fasani thought.

'Broken,' she said.

7

SOME UNKNOWABLE TIME LATER (for the light never changed inside those walls, nor did Fasani grow tired or hungry — quite as though time had no meaning at all), Sharan, with the help of her turban, succeeded in navigating many of the palace's chambers, Fasani at her side. Fasani, to her disappointment, was not able to be of much help after all, for only the domed hall in which she had first arrived seemed at all familiar to her. The rest was changed beyond recognition.

One aspect that intrigued her was the lack of corridors or passageways or any of the structures which normally linked rooms, and permitted passage in between. Instead, rooms were stuck wall-to-wall without separation; in order to reach the banqueting-hall (a richly decorated chamber with a plethora of heavy silver tables-and-chairs, and a roof open to the stars) one had to go through two bed-chambers and a library (empty, for some reason, of any actual books). Beyond the banqueting-hall was a garden, its flowers as glassy and eerily perfect as its walls, and after *that* you stepped into a humble laundry-cupboard. That was a dead-end, Sharan discovered to her chagrin ('I could have sworn there was a door on the other side here, but you see I've remembered it wrongly,' said Sharan. 'Or maybe it's changed since then.') So, back they went through the garden and the banquet-room and the bedchambers and so on.

Sharan had not exaggerated about the quantity of people wandering about. Fasani only wondered whether Sharan had not underestimated the number. At least twenty people crowded around the largest silver-wrought table in the banquet hall, stuffing themselves with delicacies which looked appetising but which did not seem to emit any fragrance at all. Heads turned as Fasani and Sharan wandered across the room and disappeared into the garden beyond, and they stared again as Fasani and Sharan wandered back. Nobody got up or tried to approach, though one man — of Fasani's own colouring, and dressed handsomely in red — lifted a hand in greeting just as she was disappearing from the room in Sharan's wake.

Nowhere did she see her sisters, or Yasmine, or Ru. Or, for that matter, Baradir.

'Who are they all?' Fasani hissed, obliged at the last moment to lower her voice, for the bedchamber that had been empty when they had passed through it two minutes before now had an occupant: a stout woman in a yellow kaftan face-down upon the bed, so deeply asleep she might have been there for hours.

'Oh, travellers,' said Sharan, intent upon her silken map. 'Wanderers. Sorcerers, one or two. Unlucky folk, gone astray somewhere between market and their homes. Sometimes all it takes is a wrong turn somewhere. Aha.' She stabbed at the etched silk with a finger, and put it away.

'Or a space appearing in the ground,' Fasani said, thinking of Baradir and how he had fallen into the sand.

'Unlucky, that,' Sharan agreed. 'Me, I was caught by curiosity; I have no one to blame but myself. I'd heard of a palace that vanished into the night, of course, but gave the tale little credence — until, one night, I saw it, from a great distance. I walked until dawn, and it was on the point of disappearing, all hazy and streaming away — but the doors opened and in I went.' She shook her head. 'Ought to have known better.'

They had proceeded by this time into a shabby, apparently disused section of the building, room after room swathed in gem-dust and curious cobwebs that shone like strings of diamond. Broken tiles covered the floors, many of them missing altogether. Every gap showed a disturbing emptiness beneath, as though the walls stood upon empty air.

Perhaps they did, thought Fasani. This was not the sort of place that much bothered about rules.

'Nobody comes here much,' said Sharan, as though the patent emptiness was not evidence enough of its abandonment. 'Not much to see, cobwebs only. And nasty spiders.' One skittered past her foot as she spoke, and she twitched the hem of her robe aside as it passed. Its legs were far too long, even for a spider, and brittle, for the *clickity-clacking* noise it made as it scurried away sounded like stone against stone. 'But,' said Sharan, more brightly, 'if there are collapsed parts of the palace, they'd be somewhere around here. You agree, yes?'

'I don't recognise any of this,' said Fasani. She tried, but the rooms she remembered fleeing through with Hanizani and Talandani resembled none of these.

'Hm.' Sharan's enthusiasm faded into a frown. 'Oh dear, what if there's a lot I know nothing about? We could be searching for a century.'

Fasani thought Sharan already had been searching for the best part of a century, but kept the thought to herself. Sharan and her map seemed the likeliest chance of escape for them all, and it wouldn't do to dishearten her.

'I wish Baradir was here,' she sighed, trailing helplessly after Sharan through another dusty, abandoned room. If she could just know that he was well, and not far away, she wouldn't so much mind being stuck in the palace for a while. 'And my sisters.'

'Is he likely to—' Sharan began, but a noise as of a heavy weight falling to the floor from some height interrupted her. She whirled, and so did Fasani.

'Ouch,' gasped Baradir.

Fasani ran to him, and fell to her knees by his side. 'You're here!' she shouted joyfully, trying to smile at him and hug him at the same time. 'I was just *wishing* for you. Oh no, are you hurt?' Having, by this time, got a good look at his face, she fell silent, staring in dismay. She swallowed. 'Baradir? What's happened to you?'

He looked like himself, but not. Half of his familiar face was unchanged; the rest was all turned to fiery-coloured glass, shattered pieces grown together to form an echo of his features. His bejewelled eye glimmered dangerously with sorcery, dark and bright, and the shaking hand he'd raised to his (apparently aching) head had not a scrap of his own skin left to it. All was brittle, shining and cold.

Baradir stared back, with no less wonder. 'Fasani?' he said in disbelief.

'Yes, it's me,' she said, beaming. 'Hanizani and Talandani are here somewhere, too, though I can't find them just at present—'

'I thought you were dead,' he breathed. 'I thought you dead, all of you, in the wreckage—'

'We got out. We thought *you* were dead, and didn't even know that you were *you* until not long ago, but then we were turned into—'

'No,' said Baradir, and thrust a hand between himself and Fasani as though to block her out. 'Too cruel. Not *this*. Any other illusion I could bear, but *not THIS*.' The final word emerged at a roar, and he hauled himself to his feet, fists clenched. 'NO MORE,' he shouted, seemingly at the ceiling. Rage blazed in good eye and glass alike, and he raised both hands, a cruel twist to his mouth, as though ready to blast the palace into oblivion.

'No!' Fasani said, and grabbed at his arm. '*Father*! I'm not an illusion! Who would have cast me, if I was? I'm real. I've been real all along.'

'Who?' echoed Baradir in a snarl. 'Why, the same sneaking, cowardly, vicious—' he stopped abruptly, and stared hard at Fasani. 'What do you mean, you've been real all along?'

Fasani tugged at his sleeve, just as she'd done as Fasee the camel. 'Got any dates?' she said, hopefully.

Baradir stared at her for so long, and in such awful silence, that she began to tremble, for the anger had not faded one whit from his face.

'Fasee?' he said at last, in a hoarse whisper.

She nodded, hope rising.

'And Hanee, and Talee...' He trailed off, and his eyes went distant with memory.

Then, to Fasani's surprise, he began to laugh. He laughed and laughed, until tears streamed from both of his eyes and he could hardly breathe.

Then he swept her up in so fierce a hug that *she* couldn't breathe either, and wept some other tears all over her head. 'What a fool I've been,' he said into her hair. 'What an idiot, what an imbecile... why, even the water-fairy couldn't make me see. I'm beyond help.'

'Completely,' agreed Fasani, smiling so hard her face hurt.

'Your sisters,' he said, abruptly releasing her. 'They're here as well? We must find them. And quickly, before *he* realises you're all here.'

'He?' said Fasani, frowning. 'Who, father?'

'Father?' interrupted Sharan, and Fasani started, having utterly forgotten her presence. 'Ah, this is why you came back? But I don't know him either.'

'Father, this is Sharan,' said Fasani. 'She's stuck here with the others. Sharan, this is Baradir bin Samar, my father. He hasn't been in here for very long either.'

'This time,' put in Baradir.

Sharan's eyes narrowed. 'Baradir... bin Samar?'

Fasani's smile widened.

'Surely not.'

'Surely *yes.*'

Sharan sat down suddenly. 'We're saved,' she said in wonder. 'After all these years, we'll be freed.'

Baradir held up a hand. 'Just a moment,' he said. 'I haven't got myself out of here either.'

'But you shall,' said Sharan. 'How can a palace contain its own creator against his will?'

'It can when it's—' began Baradir.

'Father,' said Fasani at the same time. '*Who* did you mean? About the sneak and the coward—'

'Izebadd,' said Baradir, and clutched Fasani in a protective embrace.

'*Izebadd*?' she all but shrieked.

'Izebadd,' Baradir confirmed grimly. 'Did you ever hear the tale, child? King of the Jinn, until he vanished from his throne one day, and never was heard from again.'

'*I* know it,' said Sharan. 'What about it?'

Baradir gave her a bitter quirk of a smile. 'Can you not guess?'

'No.' Sharan folded her arms. 'Not even this palace could hold a jinn-king prisoner.'

'But could a jinn-king hold a palace prisoner?'

Sharan stared.

Baradir gave a great, weary sigh. 'It was before you came,' he said to Fasani. 'Word of the might of Ibn Samar, and his damned marvellous palace, had spread so far... a tale always grows in the telling, does it not? Imagine, then, what people said of me and my sorcery, even as far away as the jinn-lands. Grossly exaggerated accounts, I've no doubt, and Izebadd took exception, for to be eclipsed in might and fame by a mere human man was (in his view) humiliating.

'He wasn't the only one who arrived here with a view to challenging me. Many others came before him. If they weren't here to try to best me, they were here to rob me — of my wealth, my ideas, anything they could get hold of. I tried to turn them out, but there were always more. And because tales of my villainy were spread with as much enthusiasm as the rest, I've no doubt I seemed like fair game. Great heroes, every one of them.' He said this with a biting scorn, and that cruel twist to his mouth. 'Anyway, Izebadd issued his challenge, and when I refused, he simply — attacked.' The anger faded from his face, leaving him only exhausted. 'I bested him — I think. But barely. And we were both destroyed by it, though I did not realise it at the time. I had to use everything I had, reach for power I'd never touched before, depths of sorcery even I could not fully master. And this was the result, though I did not realise it until much later.' He gestured at his ensorcelled face.

'As for Izebadd, I thought him vanquished, and gone. That, too, was a mistake. He was never gone. I, or I and my palace between us, had smothered him alive — in glass. Walled him up. But he wasn't dead. He was alive in there, in some fashion — and angry. After that, my own creation never missed an opportunity to hinder or harm me. Every time I fought back, whenever I reached for my own arts in defence, the glass spread deeper inside, and that's how I came to know I was cursed.' He looked down at Fasani, and managed a smile. 'Somewhere in the middle of all of that, you and your sisters arrived. I knew it wasn't safe for you here, but I had nowhere to take you, and could not simply turn you out again. Where would you have gone? I thought I could make everything right, evict Izebadd somehow — and the rest of them, too — but I underestimated the jinn-king's might. He brought half the palace down around our ears, and swamped us in sorcery...'

So much regret was there in Baradir's face, so much condemnation and loathing, that Fasani could only squeeze him again. 'It wasn't so bad, being camels,' she said.

He chuckled. 'Of all the possible outcomes, that one wasn't so bad,' he allowed.

'We've lost all your things, though,' Fasani thought it necessary to admit. 'They went into the water, I think.'

'What water— never mind. They don't matter.' He straightened. 'But we must find your sisters.'

'Yasmine, too.'

'Yasmine is here?'

'Yes. She brought us.'

'Then I owe her a great debt, and cannot yet repay it. Her son is certainly here, but I don't yet have the means of getting any of us out.'

'Who's her son?' said Sharan, clearly lost.

'Riad. He is three-quarters jinn, I believe, and Izebadd's grandson, but I do not know if that will protect him. It's my belief Izebadd is more than three-quarters mad by now.' He looked up at the ceiling again, and he developed a wary look. 'Fasani... did you say you were wishing for me?'

'Yes. I had just said, "I wish Baradir was here," and then you appeared.'

His eyes narrowed. 'Was that my own sorcery answering your wish, or some twisted idea of Izebadd's?'

'Would it answer my wish?' said Fasani.

'Of course. Your sisters', too. I made it thus, soon after you arrived.'

That explained the big, domed hall and its way of reflecting her dreams. Fasani smiled.

'In that case,' she said. 'I wish Hanizani and Talandani and Yasmine were here.' She waited, smiling. 'Oh!' she blurted guiltily. 'And Ru as well.'

'Ru—' began Baradir, but as Sharan had been before, he was interrupted by four *thuds* sounding in quick succession.

'*Ow,*' shrieked Hanizani and Talandani in unison.

Fasani rushed to help them up. Baradir went to Yasmine, and Sharan advanced upon Ru, her eyes alight with curiosity.

Fasani hugged her sisters so tight they both yelped in protest. 'Father's here,' she said.

'Your son is here,' she heard Baradir saying to Yasmine. 'And, as far as I have been able to tell, he is well.'

'Thank goodness,' sighed Yasmine.

'Also,' said Baradir, 'your father.'

'My *father*?'

Baradir led her gently over to where Fasani stood in a knot with her sisters. 'I will explain,' he said, first devoting himself to enfolding Hanizani and Talandani in a crushing embrace. 'How much do you know about his disappearance?'

'Nothing, for many years,' she answered. 'But Riad heard— he thought—'

Baradir smiled, but crookedly. 'He thought I'd done some- thing unspeakable to him, let me guess?'

Yasmine looked uncertain. 'I am afraid I did, too. It's the tale sometimes told in my lands. How the mighty Ibn Samar reached for more and more power until he challenged the jinn-king himself, and bested him, and made of him a slave…'

Baradir rolled his eyes. 'You see why I no longer wanted to be Ibn Samar?'

Yasmine said nothing, but watched him.

'No wonder you hate me.'

'I am sorry,' said Yasmine. 'I have long begun to suspect a degree of falsehood.'

'Actually,' said Baradir, 'there is some truth to that tale, but *I* was not the challenger, and while I may have enslaved him (in a sense), I did not mean to. And I heartily wish there was a way to get rid of him. Shall you hear my tale?'

'Gladly.'

So Baradir began the tale all over again.

PART THREE

Izebadd

IT CANNOT HEAR YOU, had said Izebadd's grandchild to Ibn Samar. *Not in the way that you think.*

Ha.

Well, but the child was not wrong, was he? The *palace* heard nothing, for however skilful the sorcery that powered it, a mere building it remained. Glass piled upon glass, jewels crowding upon gems, magic and enchantment bound up in an endless mess all together. A pretty thing only. Tricks. Foolery.

How he hated it.

How he had always hated it, from the moment of his first arrival. Gleaming against the cool night sky in its myriad of colours, filled with naves and fools engaged in heartless revelry; a profoundly *useless* construct. What power Ibn Samar had! And to what a use he had bent those remarkable arts!

Izebadd had wanted it for his own. He hated it, he loved it, he wanted it.

Now he had it, did not he? How long had it been his own toy, to take about with him as he chose? Empty, it had not been very amusing, but once in a while some new fool found their way inside. Watching their antics, their priceless agonies and amusements, had whiled away some few of the many, many years.

He had his favourites. The little sorceress of the turban, how amusing she was to beguile! Fancying herself so clever, with her silks and her sorcery. Setting down, as a certainty, the outlines of *his* rooms, in her absurd enchanted inks. Because of her, he had learned to shuffle the palace's many chambers like a set of wooden blocks, stacking them this way and that, confounding her attempts to lay down rules. His palace obeyed no one's rules, least of all hers.

She scarcely noticed, curse her. On she went, blithely re-drawing her foolish maps whenever a change occurred, never seeing the delicious futility of her behaviour.

She must be mad, of course.

Then there was the little carpet-trader, madder still. Smirking, and in anticipation of a high treat, Izebadd rendered up a new illusion. The process took time, for he devoted such care to the art! Every detail must be considered, must be perfect. When he had done, a new guest stood awaiting his amusements. He had created the semblance of a woman of substance, for she wore the finest silks, dyed in the most brilliant of colours. Jewels hung from her ears and her neck and glittered at her fingers and her wrists. He had made them like Sharan's, with the air of sorcery about them.

The woman herself was no beauty, but she needed no physical attractions. Izebadd set her walking through the door into the carpet-trader's room, her head held high, pride and wealth apparent with every silk-swishing step she took.

The carpet-trader stood in a knot of guests, in one corner of Izebadd's favourite dining-house. All chatter ceased when his newcomer arrived; that was always the way of it. Every closed society reacted with rapture to a new arrival.

Someone nudged the carpet-trader (a drab fellow of no amusing characteristics; Izebadd had no names for the dull ones). 'Here is a fine customer for you,' said the drab fellow, with a glint of... malice? Did the man find the carpet-trader's antics as amusing as he did?

Perhaps he was not so dull.

The trader's eyes brightened as he took in the dazzling appearance of Izebadd's new puppet.

And then, to Izebadd's high delight, off he went.

'My good lady,' said the trader, bowing so low he could almost have kissed the puppet's bejewelled sandals. 'Permit me to greet you, and bid you welcome!'

'Thank you,' Izebadd had the puppet say, coolly.

'You have travelled far, I dare say,' continued the trader. 'You will take some refreshment, and then we will choose a chamber for your own. It is the regular custom,' added the trader hastily, when the puppet made as if to turn away. 'And it will be my personal pleasure to assist in furnishing it for you...'

The trader went on in this style, which ordinarily would have pleased Izebadd inordinately. To tempt him, and tease him, with the prospect of profit, ever just out of reach... the man had nothing about him but avarice, so delicious a game—

But a distraction occurred.

It was, as ever, the work of his grandchild.

Izebadd felt a tickle, as of a feather wafted slowly over some part of his anatomy.

He had no anatomy, of course; his body, if it could be called such, was of glass now. Abandoning the carpet-trader and his puppet, he exerted his will, and narrowed his focus to the source of the tickling.

The library.

Thither he went.

'A little more,' Riad was saying, but not in his usual collected way, oh no, nothing like that. He spoke like a man under great strain, and his absurd young face reflected some exertion, for sweat rolled off him, sharp and pungent, and his teeth were gritted.

With him were his six jinn slaves. Servants, he persisted in calling them, as though the difference signified. Power was power. Izebadd would have been proud of his grandchild's achievement, were it not for his irritating insistence upon turning those six jinn's arts — and his own — upon his grandfather.

'A little more,' panted Riad.

'He is not here,' said one of the jinn, and Izebadd was delighted to note that he must soon fail under his labours. His eyes started from his head, and he was breathing like a sick horse.

'He must be!' cried Riad. 'No one cared more for learning than Izebadd! Where would he go in this cursed place, if not here?'

'He is not here,' repeated the jinn — no, a different one said it. They were all the same, these cringing, faceless creatures, contented to serve the will of another. 'We cannot release a prisoner who is not trapped, Riad.'

'He *is* trapped,' insisted Riad. 'He must be.'

'But not in here.'

Riad sighed, and collapsed into the chair Izebadd thoughtfully set for him. If he noticed that the thing had quietly removed itself from one side of the room to the other, so as to position itself within Riad's reach, he gave no sign. 'I am stumped,' he declared. 'If he's not here, then he's not anywhere, and I have no idea what to do.'

'There aren't any books,' observed one of the six faceless ones, regarding the empty crystal-glass bookshelves with doleful eye. 'A jinn wild for learning would find little to interest him here, no?'

'Why are there no books?' muttered Riad. 'That makes no sense, either.'

Izebadd, quietly, chuckled. No, it made no sense. But where would be the amusement in sensible proceedings? He had removed Ibn Samar's books himself, in the early years of his confinement. It had taken him (as near as he could reckon) ten or eleven years to thoroughly absorb the contents of them all.

Then he had hidden them.

Once in a while, he permitted one of his guests to discover one or two of them. But that game had palled some time ago.

'Perhaps Ibn Samar—' began one of the jinn-servants.

Riad's head came up, and his eyes flashed hot anger. 'What? What of Ibn Samar?'

The jinn-servant ducked his head. 'Perhaps... he may be able to locate your grandfather, and release him.'

Riad snorted. 'He imagines he will, but this is not *his* palace anymore, whatever he may say. I don't believe he can do anything with it at all. And why would he release the rival he himself entrapped?'

'Maybe he'd like his palace back,' suggested another of the servants.

'Then he should not have abandoned it in the first place.'

Abandoned. Izebadd snorted. The mighty Ibn Samar had not simply abandoned his prized creation. His "rival", King Izebadd, had forced him out of it! Sent him fleeing into the night, bested and destitute, along with every miserable nave he'd permitted to hang about the place.

Few things satisfied the soul like victory. Watching Ibn Samar disappear into the night, burdened with a curse that must kill him in time; disgraced, vanquished and despairing; oh, how Izebadd had celebrated!

True, he had at first resented his confinement to the site of their conflict. But, time reconciled one to anything, did it not? Dimly he recalled what it was once like, to have limbs like these benighted souls, and feeble fingers with no power in them at all. Now, his strong walls were his limbs, and clear windows were his eyes. He had all the magic of the palace at his beck and call, added to his own, and he would *not* be wrested from it.

One of the jinn-servants had grown bold. 'It's my belief we cannot do this without his help,' he'd just said, and Riad had turned rigid with indignation.

'We do not need that man's help,' he spat, and Izebadd felt a surprising flicker of pride; the more so when the boy added, 'I'd rather die than beg his assistance.'

The child had spirit, like his mother — and his grandmother.

Time, he thought, *to look in on Ibn Samar,* and he went at once, abandoning Riad to argument with his insubordinate henchmen.

He found the old sorcerer in the midst of a reunion, with three sparkling little females he addressed as *daughters* — and, that daughter of his own.

How had Yasmine come there?

It was enough for Riad to have pushed his way inside. Yasmine had not the right to so flout his authority.

She ought to have waited. For an invitation.

That would have been *courtesy.*

So angry was he that the floor shook, and his little group of gate-crashing guests stopped talking, and looked about themselves in alarm.

Izebadd schooled himself to patience, and let his anger fade.

The floor settled.

'He attends,' said another strange face he did not recognise, a man of the Xingqing, by his sigils and his robes.

'Who?' said one of the little daughters.

'The jinn of the palace, if I do not mistake,' said the robed one. A wide hat hung down his back, secured to his throat by a length of string.

'Izebadd.' To hear his own name spoken by Ibn Samar again, after so many years; the pain was intense, almost sweetly so. Izebadd pictured the man, torn limb from limb, his body-parts hidden in separate spots all over his own palace, and smiled to himself.

Soon.

Yasmine, his sweet, disobedient daughter, looked up and around, as though she might see him if she only tried hard enough. 'Father?' she called.

Her tone was not sweet at all. She rapped out the word, her brow thunderous, and further snapped, 'Come out, then, if you are there. It is not seemly to lurk and spy.'

Ah, how she reminded him of her mother, when she behaved like that.

'He cannot,' said the man of sigils. 'Any more than a window might detach itself from the wall, and come to join us.' His lips quirked in a faint smile at the prospect, amused by his own joke.

Sensitive, the Xingqing, and infinitely wise in the ways of sorcery.

But they did not know everything about *him*.

'Cannot I?' he said aloud to himself, and laughed.

Three minutes later, he had the satisfaction of causing a general outcry of shock, and seven people leapt back from him as he materialised before them.

One of them, he saw with glee, was his sorceress of the turban. Little Sharan, beholding for the first time the one who had for so long pulled her strings! What must she feel, and think? He did not study her face for long, because here his daughter stood, and his enemy.

'Yasmine,' he said gravely. 'I did not think to see you keeping such low company.'

She did not answer. In fact, she gave no sign of having heard him at all.

Surprised, he repeated his statement, with the same lack of result.

'Ibn Samar!' he said then, swelling in size, and speaking so loudly that the walls shook.

Well, they felt the shaking of the walls.

'Is this my father's arts?' said Yasmine to his enemy. 'Or one of yours?'

Ibn Samar stared at Izebadd in... terror? Fury?

No, nothing so flattering. He stared at his ancient enemy with — with *befuddlement,* as though Izebadd were a flower blooming out of season, or a fox with its head on backwards.

'I have never known it to manifest anything like this before,' said Ibn Samar. 'Tea-trays and sweetmeats, incense, yes. But a vase, and without the smallest need? No. Of what possible use could it be?'

A vase.

Izebadd, King of the Jinn, Vanquisher of Ibn Samar, had manifested himself as a vase.

YASMINE

'YOU ARE AWARE, I suppose,' said Yasmine softly, to Baradir, 'that your... glass is showing?'

Baradir's altered face came as little surprise to her, for she had seen it before: at the Starlight Bazaar, when she should not have been spying upon him (but had done so anyway). Then, he had revealed his true visage only briefly, for the edification of a friend — and Yasmine had caught a glimpse.

Now, whatever illusion or glamour had cloaked the strange effect was gone; worn away, perhaps, or purposely dismissed. And the curse, if it was that, had grown much worse in the scant time since. He looked a being only half man, the other half all sorcery.

'It hardly seemed worth hiding it, in here,' said Baradir, with resignation, and she saw his point at once. In fact, in *this* setting his mixed visage no longer looked so out of place as it had out in the world. Here, he fit; for who better to lord over a palace of enchanted glass but a man composed of the same?

Not that he did, anymore. Her father had usurped that role.

'It is getting worse,' she offered.

'I know.'

'What is the cause of that?'

'Using my sorcery. Even the smallest incantation is too much.' His lips twisted in a grimace. 'It has grown harder to avoid using it, of late.'

'Can nothing be done about it?'

He almost rolled his eyes, but stopped himself upon the point of it. 'Forgive me, but do you not think I've tried?'

Yasmine said no more.

It was Baradir, in the end, who broke the ensuing silence.

'We must find your son,' he said. 'But I'm afraid I offended him.'

Yasmine, unable to help herself, said: '*You*? Said something rude? I cannot think it possible.'

Baradir's mouth twitched. 'It was very rude. I suggested that it might have been *he* who enslaved his grandfather.'

'Why did you say that, when you knew it was not true?'

Baradir shrugged. 'His behaviour puzzled me. I wanted to rile him, and see what he would do.'

'And what did he do?'

'He grew angry.'

'And?'

'And left. I haven't seen him since.'

'He always had a quick temper, even as a child,' Yasmine said.

'I wonder where he gets it,' murmured Baradir.

Well, she'd deserved that. '*And*,' she said firmly, 'he was always fascinated by tales of his illustrious grandfather — and, specifically, what had become of him. As such, he was fascinated by tales of you, too. I thought he would grow out of both, but he did not. If he is here, he'll be trying to find Izebadd.'

'And free him, I imagine. Which is why we must find him. If we are all here with the same purpose, we ought not to be impeding one another.'

'He's powerful.'

'So you've said.'

'If he does not wish to be found—'

'Pardon me,' said a new voice, and Yasmine whirled.

She saw, gathered in a knot in one corner of the dusty, disused room, Baradir's three daughters, engaged in some animated discourse of their own; Ru, standing not far away, intently studying some aspect of the palace's construction, and quite oblivious; and, near the door, the turbaned woman, Sharan, with a stranger.

No; not a stranger.

'Zod?' she said, and went nearer.

Zod — for it was he who'd spoken — nodded, and bowed. 'My... master has sent me to you,' he said.

He'd hesitated. Why? She watched him through narrowed eyes, and said: 'He did no such thing, did he?'

Abashed, Zod looked away.

'Who's his master?' murmured Baradir, at her elbow.

'Riad. This is one of his... servants.' Now it was her turn to hesitate.

Baradir did not miss it, either. 'Servants?' he echoed, with a sidelong glance.

'I am not perfectly certain they aren't slaves,' she admitted. 'I do not think Riad would do such a thing, but if he thought the cause urgent enough...'

'Rescuing his grandfather might be seen as such.'

'In his eyes, yes.'

A swift, sharp look from Baradir. 'Not in yours?'

She hesitated, again, and instead of answering addressed herself to Zod. 'You know where my son is?'

'I do, and I have come to beg you to attend him.'

'Why?'

'He... over-extends himself, and requires aid.'

'My father is a match for him, is he?'

'Your father is a match for all of us.'

'Even imprisoned under glass. Yes, he would be.' Viewed in that light, the wreck of Baradir's person was no mystery. More of a surprise that he'd survived the encounter at all.

Just how powerful *was* Ibn Samar, anyway? He'd protested that the stories of his exploits — good and bad — were much exaggerated, and perhaps they were.

But not in every particular.

'We need no entreaty,' said Yasmine to Zod. 'We had been considering the problem of how to find him, so your arrival is most welcome. Take us to him.'

Zod bowed again, and immediately turned away.

But on the point of following him, Sharan detained her with a touch to her elbow. 'Are we trusting this one?' she said.

'He is familiar to me.' She did not add, that her anxiety for her son was growing beyond bearing; that she would brave worse dangers than a tumble-down palace possessed by the mad shade of her too-powerful father in order to see him, and assure herself of his well-being.

'You are certain?' said Sharan. 'There is something odd about that man.'

'Zod? He is a jinn, and not a man at all. To my knowledge, there isn't a scrap of humanity about him.'

'That might explain it,' admitted Sharan.

'Might?'

But Sharan only shook her head. 'There are... it is not the first time I've seen peculiarities like his, in these halls.'

'What peculiarities?' Yasmine demanded, for she grew impatient. Riad needed her, and — in a more obscure way — so did her father. So did Baradir, and his daughters. The sooner all these disparate problems were resolved, the sooner peace could be restored.

'I cannot explain them. There is something *off*, that is all.'

'We will be cautious.'

'That must content me.'

Yasmine looked towards the door, where Zod stood paused upon the threshold, waiting with a serene patience she found as reassuring as Sharan's apprehensions were disturbing.

'I have to go,' she said, more to Baradir than anybody else.

'I understand,' he said. 'I'd go, too.'

She gave him a quick, grateful smile.

'But,' he added. 'Sharan is right. This is a place full of tricks and changefulness — and hatred. I don't recognise my own creation anymore, for it is become Izebadd's, and he is mad.'

'You think this some trick of his?'

'I think it possible,' said Baradir.

Yasmine considered. 'Then I will go alone.'

'No.'

'On no account must we take your daughters.'

'On no account in the world,' he agreed. 'I must care for them. But — will you take Ru?'

Unable immediately to detect what had become of Ru, Yasmine saw him at last — floating upon a coil of mist-carpet not far from the ceiling, intent upon some section of the wall. He had conjured colour out of the dull glass, and she did not think it was merely a wiping-away of the dust that had done it. Where his hands passed, light brightly shone, and left scintillating colour in its wake.

'Interesting,' said Baradir, following her gaze.

'He is here to study,' she said. 'I promised he might do so, if he helped us to find our way here.'

Baradir sighed. 'No secret of mine has ever been honoured, has it? But *he* I will forgive, since he has restored my daughters to me.'

'Ru?' called Yasmine.

She had to repeat his name twice more before he heard, and then, with only a small show of reluctance, he came wafting down to the ground again. 'Yes?' he said, looking from Yasmine to Baradir. 'This is remarkable,' he said to the latter, before Yasmine could speak. 'Truly remarkable. Far more so than I expected! Even the tales, extravagant though they are, do it no justice.' He eyed Baradir for a moment, and said further: 'I am wondering, then, if the stories have done *you* justice.'

'Extravagant though they are?' said Baradir, with a faint smile.

'Just so.'

'I will share with you every detail of my methods,' said Baradir, 'if you will help us to evict the jinn-king Izebadd from within these walls.'

Ru's eyes widened. 'But he is your father,' Ru said to Yasmine.

'Yes,' she said.

'And you lend yourself to this plan?'

'Why should I not?'

Ru was silent with surprise. 'Why, it will mean his end. His body is long gone. If he lives still, it is Ibn Samar's sorcery who keeps him alive. Remove that, and...' He spread his hands.

Sharan, her arms folded with some unexpressed indignation, said, 'And good riddance to him. Begging your pardon,' with an inclination of her head to Yasmine, 'but if it is *he* who keeps us here, I'd as soon see him gone.'

Yasmine bit her lip. 'His time is long past,' she said softly. 'And he is — dangerous. He cannot be permitted to continue his persecution of Sharan, and the others here.'

Ru said, 'I accept the bargain.'

'I will go along,' said Sharan.

Baradir nodded. 'Be wary,' he said.

'What shall you do?' asked Yasmine.

Baradir looked over at where his daughters still stood in discussion. 'Look for Izebadd. And if I am not much mistaken, the girls have been hatching some plan to that effect.'

Yasmine said nothing further, acknowledging his words with only a brief touch to his arm. She would have left, then, but Baradir suddenly leaned much nearer, and whispered for her ears alone: 'Sharan is right. There is a deal of sorcery surrounding the one you called Zod, and I do not know if it is his.'

'What?' Yasmine barely prevented herself from staring like an idiot at Zod; Baradir spoke in confidence for a reason. 'How can you tell?'

'I've an unusual eye.' He did not elaborate; now was not the time. 'Have a care,' he recommended. 'I fear you may run into Izebadd sooner than I do.'

'So much the better,' she said coldly. 'I have one or two things to say to him.'

'Remember that he... is not the father you once knew, anymore.' Baradir squeezed her fingers, briefly, and moved away.

Yasmine wanted to protest that he would never hurt *her,* any more than he would have hurt her mother. But Baradir was right. The Izebadd of the palace, she did not know, and never had.

Gathering her courage, she concealed her unease behind a lifted chin and a confident stride, and followed Zod to the door. 'Forgive our slowness,' she said. 'We are ready to see Riad now.'

Zod, expressionless, bowed, and left the room without saying a word.

Yasmine, with Ru and Sharan behind her, followed him back into the depths of the palace.

Riad

'WAIT,' SAID RIAD, STOPPING dead in the process of exiting the pointless library. 'Where's Zod?'

His remaining jinn looked blankly back at him, five of them only, and of what use could five be when six hadn't been enough? 'We don't know,' said Sidah, helpfully.

'*Well,*' said Riad. 'How long has he been gone? At least tell me that much.'

But they couldn't, any more than Riad could himself. He supposed that meant they had been too busy with the task he'd assigned to them to pay much heed to their colleague, and he further supposed he ought not to be angry with them for it.

Still, the disappearance of Zod was a complication, yet another one. He thought back to the glorious day when he'd seen Ibn Samar's famous palace glimmering on the horizon, and recognised it for what it was. His elation *then* seemed all the more absurd *now,* when the dream-palace had proved a nest of nightmares, and he was no nearer to extricating his grandfather than when he'd first set foot over the threshold.

'Can we find him?' he said, keeping rein on his temper only by supreme effort of will.

'I shouldn't think so,' said one of them.

'Why not?' He growled something more, and rubbed futilely at his forehead; the gesture did nothing for his headache, of course. 'You get the *best* people, and they tell you—'

'Because he is mine, now,' continued... one of them.

Riad stared at each of the five in turn. They looked too similar, damn them, as though they thought that cladding themselves in similar forms would somehow please him. A row of pleasant-faced men and women, their black hair swept up in turbans (for the men) or bound with scarves (the women), and even *colour-coordinated,* would you believe it: red sirwal and coat for Mabbi, yellow for Reqad, Sidah in sea-blue, black for Kezahd, orange for Ariza. All of them met his gaze, unabashed. And, irritatingly, bemused.

'Who said that?' demanded Riad.

All five of them silently shook their heads.

'But if it was not *you,* then who was it? There's no one else here.' Riad looked around, even checked behind the half-open door, but found nobody.

'I did,' came the voice again, and if Riad could have credited the idea at all, he might have said the words came from a large vase standing upon a velvety red rug in the centre of the room...

'Wait,' he said. 'How long has that been there?'

None of his jinn answered, and neither did the vase. It stood inert, as a vase should, even if it was an unusually splendid specimen: almost man-high, made inevitably from stained glass (a sojourn in Ibn Samar's abode was enough to cure anyone of an admiration for that art), and possessed of a fine spray of amber-coloured lilies, all of them enormous.

And, Riad saw when he got closer, all of them fake. They weren't amber-coloured, they were amber-wrought.

He lifted a finger, and flicked at the petals of the nearest of them. *Ting.*

'That,' said the vase gravely, 'is bad manners.'

Riad jumped back. 'Right,' he said furiously. 'I've had it with this place. Talking vases! It's the outside of enough.'

'Oh?' said the vase with interest. 'What are you going to do about it?'

'Why, I'll—' Riad stopped, finding the question unanswerable.

The vase looked smug, if a vase could; shone all the brighter, as though freshly polished; and drew itself up to its full five-foot-something height. 'As I was saying,' it said. 'Zod is mine now.'

Riad, greatly daring, approached the vase again, and peeped inside.

Empty, save for the long, slender stems of the bejewelled lilies. No Zod.

'Oh?' he said, mimicking the vase's own cool contempt. 'And what are you going to do with him?'

The lilies flexed their petals, and shivered, the clacking of the cold amber-stone curiously reminiscent of laughter. 'I am playing a game,' confided the vase.

'And who are the other players, fortunate souls that they must be?' said Riad, all acid.

'You know them.'

'Do I? I think not.' But he knew Ibn Samar to be loose somewhere in the palace, and might not the vase refer to him?

Who else would the sorcerer's own household wares want to play with?

'Your charming mother,' said the vase instead.

'What?' gasped Riad.

'She's grown handsomer than ever,' continued the vase, with... pride?

'She cannot be here,' insisted Riad.

'Cannot she? Why?'

'Because—' Again, Riad could find no answer. Seething, he spat, 'You are playing a game with *me*, aren't you?'

The jewel-flowers chortled. 'I am playing a game with all of you.'

'I dare say it's very amusing.'

'I haven't been so well entertained in years!'

'One doesn't expect a vase to be up to much, by way of entertainment.'

This, for some reason, angered the vase, for it swelled with indignation, almost to the point of explosion. 'I am *not* a vase!' it roared.

Riad folded his arms, and stared long and hard at the thing. 'Looks like a vase to me. How about you?' he said to his five remaining jinn.

'Most vase-like,' confirmed Ariza.

'Absolutely the most vase-shaped vase I've seen,' added Reqad.

'Could be nothing else,' put in Kezahd.

'It could be something else!' shrieked the vase. '*It is!*'

'Such as?' said Riad. 'Go on, prove it. If you aren't a vase, let's see your real form.'

The vase, visibly, tried. It stretched and strained, but nothing much happened. At length, with an ominous tinkling of broken glass, the lilies disappeared. All that remained was a vase — empty, and hollowly echoing.

'There,' it said, panting. 'What now am I?'

'A vase,' said Riad.

A shattering roar of frustration followed. Riad, stubborn, stood his ground.

'Let's get back to the matter of Zod,' he said. 'What have you done with him?'

'He is mine,' said the vase darkly.

'Actually, he's mine. Bound in service until it pleases *me* to release him—'

'And Zod,' said Mabbi helpfully.

'Yes, yes. Still, release must be negotiated, do you understand? You cannot simply take him from me, without either his leave or mine, and therefore—'

'Did you have his leave?' interrupted Ariza. She was addressing the vase.

'Of course,' said the vase, airily.

'You lie,' said Riad.

'Maybe. You cannot know.'

'I'd like him back,' said Riad, dismissing this point. 'Let him go.'

'No.'

'Really, it is too much for my servants to be held hostage by household crockery!'

'I will take you in his place,' said the vase, in a sly tone.

Riad blinked. 'What?'

'You,' repeated the vase.

'No!'

'Are you sure?'

'Perfectly! The whole question is ridiculous.'

Silence.

Then, Sidah vanished in a flurry of sea-blue cloth.

'How about you for the two of them?' said the vase.

Riad's fists slowly clenched. 'You'll give her back, too.'

Mabbi went next, winking out like a red lamp.

'Three for one,' said the vase. 'A good deal, by anybody's standards.'

'Master...' said Ariza, drawing nearer to Kezahd. 'Do something.'

It did not save her. Moments later she, too, was gone, and then Kezahd, and Riad was alone in the disused library with the vase.

'All six, then,' said the vase, in an affable tone which made Riad long to smash it. 'Give yourself up, and I'll give them up.'

Somewhere in the midst of Riad's growing fury, a question bubbled up, and grew. He drew a slow breath. 'Why,' he said with forced calm, 'did you not just swipe me to begin with?'

'Well, because...' said the vase. 'Because... it is more fun this way.'

'More *fun*? For who?!'

The vase growled. 'I want you to come *willingly*.'

'This is your idea of willing! Have you never heard of coercion?'

'Curse you, are you coming or not?' roared the vase.

'Fine!' Riad screamed back. 'Let my jinn go and I'll play your stupid game!'

Zod reappeared first with a *pop,* and stood looking confused. 'Master?' he said, blinking.

'Hello, Zod. Welcome back.'

Next came Sidah, then Reqad and Mabbi and Ariza and Kezahd. They looked, to Riad's temporary relief, unharmed and unchanged.

He had not much time to congratulate himself on these reassuring facts, for with a cheery *pop* of his own, he felt himself turned head-down, and whisked somewhere away.

Bested by a vase, was his last thought. *Mother must never find out about this, or I'll never—*

Consciousness faded, taking his embarrassment with it.

❦

'Riad!' came mother's salutation, followed by a pair of arms and a warm, mother-scented body engulfing him.

Riad, speechless with chagrin, submitted to this greeting in wordless indignation.

'And what did you mean by disappearing like that!' she said, moments later, upon releasing him. Her face, half relief, half anger, was turned to his.

'There's a pair of sorcerers behind you,' said Riad.

'Yes. Ru, Sharan, this is my wayward child.'

Ru made a bow, and a greeting, which Riad had courtesy enough to return. 'The one you sought,' said Ru.

'Yes,' snapped Yasmine.

'If I had set eyes on him as a stranger only,' said Sharan, 'I would have said he was jinn. Like that other one.'

'I am,' said Riad, and sighed, for Yasmine still looked as much thunderous as anything. 'You knew where I was,' he told her.

'In a dangerous, disappearing palace, without assistance or aid, and also without power of exit. Yes.'

'And now,' he growled, 'so are you. First-rate. Was I supposed to ignore the place, and grandfather too?'

'You mistake,' said Yasmine, more calmly. 'I do not object to your coming here. I object to your leaving me behind. And I believe you to be labouring under some misapprehensions.'

That silenced him, at least for a moment. 'And where are we come to?' he said, letting his mother's words pass. His glance about had revealed no vase, to his secret relief; perhaps his mother need know nothing about it. In fact, he saw nothing of any note at all. The four of them stood in a simple, square room, the walls and floor and ceiling of which were dark, opaque glass, and without any adornment. Or furniture. Or door. Like a space waiting to become a room, Riad thought.

'I can't determine,' said Yasmine. 'We were fetched by Zod, out of concern for you, or so he said. *Have* you been over-extending yourself?'

'Yes,' said Riad bluntly. 'But Zod wouldn't care about that.'

'Why not?'

'They do as I tell them.'

'And cannot, therefore, have thoughts of their own?' she said drily, with that twitch of the lips he sometimes hated, because it meant she was quietly laughing at him.

'They're loyal, but they don't *care*. Not like that.'

'Well, I will not contest that point with you. But if Zod did not fetch us to assist you, why then did he?'

They grew uncomfortably close to the subject of the obnoxious vase, and Riad hesitated, unsure how to successfully skirt it. 'What colour was he wearing?' he said.

'Zod?' She frowned in thought. 'I don't recall.'

'Indigo,' said Sharan. 'Very good silk.'

'Then it wasn't Zod. He wears green, and none of them wear very good silk.'

Yasmine gave a soft, exasperated sigh. 'It seems you were right, Sharan. A fine trap we've stepped into.'

'And who,' said she, 'would know to use your son's well-being as the bait?'

'So perfect an illusion,' put in Ru, in his quiet way, 'must be the work of the jinn.'

'I know it,' said Yasmine grimly. 'How were you brought here, Riad?'

'I'd... rather not say.'

She merely looked at him.

'Fine. The safety of my servants was threatened.'

That this surprised her was evident, and he felt chagrined again. Did she think he cared nothing for his subordinates?

'It must be... surely, it must be my father,' said Yasmine. 'Who else could manage it — and who else would want to lure the two of us apart, in particular? But then...'

'Then he is not a prisoner in some forgotten corner of the palace,' said Riad. 'Not popped in a box and the lid nailed shut, as I'd thought.'

'No. He must be very aware, and... and active.'

Riad was silent in consternation, thinking of everything he and his jinn had done since their arrival. Had his stealthy grandfather been aware of all of that? Had he watched and listened to (and, doubtless, laughed over) their fruitless efforts to find him?

'*Why* a vase, grandfather?' he said aloud, and loudly. 'Of all the forms to take, why that one? A great king, in so menial a guise! It's sloppy.'

'What vase— *oh.*' She shook her head, her eyes wide with realisation. 'In the room, with us! And all the things we said—' she broke off, as the vase in question — Riad was beginning to find it grossly ugly, by now — quietly manifested in the middle of the room, and sat there, attempting elegance. 'Father,' said Yasmine sharply. '*What* are you doing?'

'I wondered when you would catch on,' said the vase, smugly.

But Ru, hitherto a watchful presence behind Yasmine, now darted forward with a speed he hardly looked capable of. He gripped the top edge of the vase with both hands, a strong, white-knuckled hold, his face grim.

The vase shattered into a thousand pieces, which rained all over the stark floor with a melodious *tinkling* sound.

'Ru,' said Yasmine, in a dangerously quiet voice. 'What have you done?'

'Wait,' he said softly.

Riad, stifling a desire to break *Ru* into a thousand pieces, schooled himself to patience, and waited.

The glass pieces turned to powder, first, and wafted away.

Then, in the blink of an eye, another vase stood where the old one had been, almost identical in appearance, though with perhaps an altered array of colours.

'There,' said Ru. 'It is involuntary, I think.'

'You mean he's a vase because he cannot be anything else?' said Yasmine.

'Precisely.'

'I've said it before,' said Riad. 'But *why* a vase?'

The vase, though, was silent and still, and had nothing to say for itself.

'He cannot talk, perhaps, upon first appearance,' said Yasmine, eyeing the vase with something like interest. 'He was silent before.'

'Manifestation takes considerable power,' said Ru. 'All that he has, at first. It is remarkable that he can achieve it at all, let alone repeatedly.'

'And a vase, because...?' said Yasmine.

Ru shrugged. 'I have no explanation for that.'

Sharan considered the vase with palpable disfavour. 'I would say that he must like vases, but that cannot be. This one is in such poor taste.'

'He never had any interest in trinkets,' said Yasmine. 'Except as they demonstrated his wealth.'

All four looked at the ugly vase in silence.

'Involuntary,' Yasmine agreed. 'He really isn't himself.'

'If I may be permitted,' said Ru, with a diffidence Riad had not hitherto noticed in him. 'Ibn Samar and Izebadd are... neither of them themselves, now.'

'What does that mean?' demanded Riad. 'You've seen Ibn Samar, have you?'

Yasmine said, with marked coolness, 'Why? Have you?'

'I've seen him,' Riad growled, his fists clenching.

'Then doubtless you were extremely rude.'

'He was extremely rude to me!'

'Well, he did confess as much,' said Yasmine fairly.

Riad blinked at her. 'What? What can you know of him?'

'I—'

'If I *may*,' interrupted Ru. 'His Majesty Izebadd is in some sorcerous distress, clearly. His arts are as entangled as he is himself. He is still unthinkably powerful, but in a way that is... twisted about, and—'

'Broken?' supplied Yasmine.

'Yes. In a way.'

'Baradir said the same. Of himself.'

Ru inclined his head. 'Precisely. We cannot know what Izebadd intended to make of himself, but he has turned out as a vase instead. Twice. And as for Baradir, he is sparing with his sorcery, for so powerful a man, and I suspect him of holding more than one reason for his reticence.'

'That creeping glass,' said Yasmine.

'That is likely one of them.'

'And you think his sorcery is going awry?'

'Yes. For a long time, I imagine. The more so—' here Ru's gaze returned to the vase in their midst, '—the longer he remains in this palace.'

'And the same is true of father, now that Baradir's here,' said Yasmine. 'They make each other worse, in short.'

Ru smiled at her, the smile of a scholar alight with an idea. 'It is only a notion. But I think that ill-advised battle of theirs forged an unhealthy bond between them, and they are both suffering under it still.'

A muffled shattering noise obscured the end of Ru's sentence, the shattering of splintered glass, and Riad looked sharply at the vase. It remained intact, but having done its best to explode, its surface was riddled with deep cracks.

An inarticulate muttering emanated from it, a sound which grew in volume and clarity until the vase was delivering itself of invective at an ear-shattering volume. 'Make me into a vase, will he! I will kill him! Rend him! Turn *him* into glass, see how *he* likes it, and smash him to bits—'

'He *is* turning into glass, Father,' interrupted Yasmine, at a volume Riad had never heard her use before. 'Which, I collect, is your doing, as much as your current predicament is his. It is useless for you to blame each other, for you have both been at fault, and you have both suffered for it. So you'd better fix it, hadn't you? BOTH OF YOU.'

Her tirade gained in vehemence until she drowned out even the vase, her words rolling through the room like thunder, and crackling off the walls.

Riad, in spite of himself, flinched, and quietly hoped this side of his mother's personality would never be turned upon her son. She looked like a desert storm incarnate, positively ablaze with anger— no, indeed, he did not exaggerate; those *were* arcane flames wreathing her fingers, and scorching up her arms.

'This cursed *palace*,' she spat, uncontested now, for the vase that was his grandfather had at last fallen silent — perhaps in astonishment, to equal Riad's. 'It has obsessed Baradir to the point of his own doom, and my father too, and then my son as well—'

'No,' said Riad indignantly. 'I never cared a button for the palace, only for the fact that grandfather was here—'

'Your *reason*,' shouted Yasmine, 'is immaterial, for the outcome is the same. Don't you see? This palace might be a marvel, and beautiful beyond imagining, but it's a curse upon all who set eyes on it.' She took a deep, steadying breath, and the arcane fire receded. 'It has to go,' she said, more softly, and her eyes widened, as though she were taken aback by her own words.

'Go?' echoed Riad. 'You can't mean that.'

'But I do. It is not only Izebadd who needs to be liberated from its allure, or his prisoners who must be freed from the confines of its walls.' She looked at Sharan as she spoke, whose face betrayed a growing disquiet. 'All of us are trapped. All of us are cursed, the more so with every minute we spend here. It *must go.*'

Sharan said quietly, 'No one can be more eager to leave than me, but — but — must it come to that? The world will never again see its like.'

'Nor should it,' said Yasmine, grim as night, and unmoved.

She looked, for some reason, at Ru.

He walked to the nearest wall, and laid a hand against it, quite tenderly. Looking up at the shining glass of the ceiling sloping overhead, his face sad, he said: 'Perhaps you are right.'

'Well,' said the vase, in a cool way. 'If you want to destroy my palace, child, you must first get past me.' The words were spoken with a mildness at odds with his earlier rage, but an underlying grimness made of them a direct challenge.

'Won't you reconsider, Father?' said Yasmine. 'You cannot have been happy here.'

'No.'

'Then,' she said, and drew herself up. 'We'll do as we must. Either you release your grip on this cursed place, Father, or we will bring it down around your ears — and you with it.'

Baradir

'Father,' said Hanizani gravely. 'We've been thinking.'

'So I see,' said Baradir, with a trace of unease, for his three girls had arranged themselves before him like a little wall, which could only be passed by great finesse. Or total obedience.

'This place,' she continued, casting a quick — contemptuous? — glance around at the dust-shrouded room. 'It needs to be...'

'Got rid of,' said Talandani, when her sister hesitated.

'Yes,' said Hanizani.

Baradir blinked. 'Got... got rid of?' he echoed weakly. 'But—'

'It's best not to argue,' said Talandani serenely.

'But—'

'It's destroyed you.'

'I—'

'It's almost killed us.'

'Well— but— it was not the *palace* that did that, Talandani. It was—'

'You, the palace and the jinn-king between you.' Her expression became stony, and he found himself fixed with an unforgiving stare.

'The jinn-king must be got rid of, too,' said Hanizani.

'And me?' said Baradir, looking from one to the other. 'Must I also be got rid of?'

He did not quite like the look his two elder daughters exchanged. 'We talked of it,' said Talandani.

'We were *camels,*' said Hanizani, with a flash of anger. 'For years and years and years.'

'I am so sorry,' he said. 'More sorry than I can— I never meant for— I didn't *know.*'

Fasani, at last, broke her unusual, grave silence. 'Oh, stop it,' she chided. 'We are not getting rid of Father and it's cruel to torment him.'

'He deserved it,' said Talandani. 'A little.'

'Yes, and now you've finished,' said Fasani firmly.

Talandani looked more amused than abashed, but she said no more.

'So,' said Baradir meekly. 'I'm to be permitted to go on?'

'Yes, but the palace must not,' said Hanizani.

'What if I could... mend it?' he tried.

'Can you?'

Three pairs of eyes stared at him, uncompromising.

'I... don't know,' he said. 'May I try?'

Hanizani folded her arms. 'What do you mean by *mend it*?' she demanded. 'What will it be like when you're finished?'

'Well, Izebadd will be gone.'

'Mm. And how are you going to do that?'

'It was our thought,' put in Fasani, 'that if you destroy the palace, it would destroy the jinn-king, too.'

Baradir, chilled to hear such ruthless notions emerging from the mouth of his youngest child, could only stare.

'Well, wouldn't it?' she said.

'Likely.'

'Very good. Then we know what to do.' Her small face was a picture of grim resolve.

Baradir did not like that either.

'Dear child,' he said. 'Please, consider. Perhaps Izebadd does not deserve to die?'

'*We almost died,*' she said. 'And some other people *did.*'

'And both of us are eternally at fault for that, yes. But if I deserve a reprieve, why does not my enemy also?'

Fasani's face darkened. 'You tried to kill him yourself,' she pointed out. 'That's how he got stuck in here in the first place.'

'Yes. And every terrible thing that's happened since has been a consequence of that ill-starred battle. I want no more of it, Fasani.'

Abandoning her bloodthirsty plans with a tiny sigh, Fasani looked up at her sisters. 'He is as stubborn as you, Hani.'

'Well, perhaps he is right,' she allowed.

'Thank you,' said Baradir gravely.

'What, then?' said Hanizani. 'Do you have any idea how to dislodge him?'

'I am working on that part,' said Baradir, only half knowing what he said, for his attention was at that moment distracted. Creeping up from the floor and wreathing around Fasani's feet, an odd shimmer in the air betrayed the presence of potent sorcery — the same aura he had detected surrounding the jinn-servant who'd fetched Yasmine away. It could have been the jinn's own magic, he had allowed, having no way to say for certain that it was not.

But Fasani had no magic.

'No,' he said grimly to the air, startling his daughters. 'You shall not have any of these three.' He wound his own sorcery about them as he spoke, weaving a net to hold them with; a gust of air to clear away the intruding enchantment; a tether to keep them near.

Something, close by, snarled.

And fought. *Something,* with a might to match his own, tore at his tethers and his net, centring upon Fasani.

He gritted his teeth, and held, every nerve strained with the effort of holding them close and safe.

'Father,' said Hanizani. 'What is it?'

'It's Izebadd,' said Fasani.

'Yes,' gasped Baradir.

'How discourteous,' said his youngest child. 'When we have just settled it that he shan't be killed! I wish I had never agreed to it.'

To Baradir's surprise, the pressure upon his sorcerous wards abruptly ceased, from one breath to the next. A heavy silence fell, a cessation of hostilities as inexplicable as it was welcome. Baradir waited, tense and alert, for some fresh attack.

None came.

'That vase,' said Hanizani.

'It's like the one that was here before,' said Talandani, frowning.

'It is the same,' said Baradir, for if ever a vase could be said to loiter with an air of innocence, then this one was doing exactly that. It sat three feet away, tall and elegant and innocuous, for all the world as though it had been there all along.

Baradir, frowning, shook his head. 'Come, Majesty,' he said. 'Why a vase, now?' He winced, and strove to hide it — too slow, for Hanizani gave him a sharp look. The invasive chill of new glass set him shivering, creeping inexorably through his torso. Soon it would claim both his arms, he knew, and—

'Father,' said Fasani, ignoring the vase. 'Your face.'

He put up a hand to feel for himself, though he did not need to; the icy, brittle sensation engulfing his formerly healthy cheek and jaw told him the glass had spread there, too.

So little sorcery as he had expended, really, with such results. It had been so, ever since he had set foot in his palace again; as though his own ensorcelled glass, the constructs by which he had raised these glittering walls, were reaching out to claim him.

'Never mind it, Fasani,' he murmured, keeping his eyes on the vase.

Fasani turned her displeasure upon the vase, too. 'You did that,' she said, and kicked it. '*And* you made me into a camel,' she added, and delivered another kick.

The vase's smooth surface splintered with a horrific crunching noise — and then smoothly reformed itself to an unblemished finish.

Baradir did not think any of it was the result of Fasani's kicking.

'Fasani,' he said, and quietly drew her away from the vase. 'All of you, please stay back from our... guest.'

The vase, somehow, bristled, and abruptly spat, in a voice Baradir distantly recognised: 'Guest?' He repeated the word, at volume, and it rang and boomed about the room.

'Prisoner?' suggested Hanizani, politely.

'You are *my* prisoners!'

'I am sure it's very amusing to keep prisoners,' said Fasani reflectively. 'Did you ever have any before, Father?'

Baradir, thinking swiftly back to his much earlier life, thought it best not to answer this question.

'I think prisoners are wearisome,' said Talandani. 'Especially this one.'

'Yes, it would be far nicer to have our house to ourselves again,' agreed Hanizani.

'Girls—' said Baradir, uneasy, for though the vase looked innocuous he knew exactly what kind of power lay at the disposal of King Izebadd. Carefully, he extended his sorcery again, consolidating his grip on his daughters. If the jinn-king raised so much as a flicker of sorcery against them, he would know of it.

'Why don't you just go?' said Fasani.

'Go?' said the vase, in blank disbelief. 'This is my palace! I shall never give it up.'

'Why?' said Fasani. 'Just because Father made it?'

'Pitiful,' said Talandani, with all the withering contempt at her disposal.

The vase swelled. 'I won it, by right of combat—'

'Did you?' said Talandani. 'And yet, it's Father who walked away free, and you who stayed... here.'

'Stuck,' said Fasani.

'Your father has not been free,' said the vase icily.

Baradir said, softly, 'We both lost, Izebadd.'

'And you shall lose again,' said the vase. 'You should not have come back. Nor should you have brought me these new prisoners to enjoy.'

'Your daughter brought them,' said Baradir. 'In point of fact. Shall you so defy her, as to harm them?'

'Why not? She defies me.'

'We did decide not to kill you,' said Fasani kindly. 'That must count for something.'

'Why did you decide that?' Baradir might have expected more anger, and more coldness, but the vase — Izebadd — sounded... interested.

'Father said not.'

'I know. Why did you listen?'

'I suppose he's right.'

Izebadd said nothing, for a while. Baradir wondered what might be turning through his disordered mind, and could not guess at it.

'I could crush you,' said Izebadd at length. 'Like insects.'

'And shall you?' said Hanizani.

There came no reply; not then, and not at all.

Izebadd's response came wordlessly, and painfully. Taken unawares, Baradir, engulfed in arcane fire, fought to breathe; dark flame roared around him, obscuring his sight, smoke choking his lungs.

'Fasani!' he shouted, as his hair caught, and began to burn. 'Girls!'

Whether they responded or not, he could not know, for the roar of fire drowned every other sound.

Cursing, his nose filled with the acrid scent of his own clothes burning, Baradir reached for his sorcery. All of it.

Water, icy-cold and shocking, poured from the ceiling, and drenched him.

The flames went out with a *cough*.

He stood dripping, chest heaving, unwilling to move, for he was glass to his fingertips now, and the chill was creeping down to his legs.

'Father,' said Fasani, and would have run to him, her face alive with concern.

'No,' he said, holding up both his hands to stop her, and Hanizani and Talandani; all three stood gazing in blank dismay, and he knew then that he was lost.

At least they had been spared Izebadd's attack. It seemed the only person to be crushed like an insect was Baradir himself.

That was fair.

And then, another attack. The world expanded, all in a rush, leaving Baradir dizzy, and he saw the room from an impossible position an inch from the floor. His daughters loomed over him, fascinated and appalled, and there was no *space*, he could neither move nor breathe, for everything that he was now occupied a space no larger than... than a pebble. He was become a pebble, and the pressure of so brutal a confinement beat murderously upon him.

Every inch of him shrieked in agony.

With a roar, he burst the enchantment, and was cannoned forth with a velocity that threw him face-down onto the floor.

He lay there, trembling and coughing, but himself again, and the pain slowly ebbed.

He was cold, colder than ever. Cold from his forehead to his toes, shivering so hard that his teeth clacked together with a sound like polished gems tumbling in a bowl.

When he looked up, he saw a world traced in arcane light and sorcerous shadow; the colours too brilliant, the darkness too dark. He blinked; his vision blurred; but no tears seeped from his glass-shrouded eyes.

His girls came forward. He did not have the energy to prevent them, anymore, and they did not appear to be in danger. The jinn-king contented himself with Baradir's torment alone.

'Father,' whispered Fasani, and went to her knees beside him. He passed a hand over his eyes, rubbed uselessly at them, unable to see the warm, living girls he loved. His youngest daughter was an indistinct shape etched in brilliance; his eldest, two silhouettes against the light.

It was the palace, he realised. So drowned in sorcery was it, so steeped in mesmerising magic, it smothered everything else. A mere life, a mortal, was as a guttering candle to the desert sun.

Except for Baradir, now. He alone blazed at the heart of his creation, for the same ensorcelled stuff that made up its beloved and despised walls now formed his own limbs, his own eyes, his own heart.

'I am well,' he tried to tell his daughters, and the words emerged oddly too: they echoed and rang, not melodically, and he winced.

'You are not!' wept Fasani. 'Look what he's done to you!' He perceived, dimly, that her small fists were bunched, and the shifting colours of her form roiled dangerously.

Baradir, glancing down at his own self, noted — not without interest — that his clothes were no longer fashioned of cloth and leather and stitching. He lay wreathed in arcane smoke, not dissimilar to that which Ru used to fly. The general outline of a robe clad his torso, and his legs; his arms sported sleeves of swirling mist.

He tried to sit up, tried to comfort his daughters, but he dared not touch them. What might happen if he did, with these altered hands? He was a creature of sorcery now, and there was no telling what fresh disasters he would wreak.

'You must not be angry,' he said, as gently as he could. 'I did this to myself, you know.'

'You didn't,' said Talandani, and even her cool manner was gone; the words dripped ice. 'Izebadd attacked you. We *saw*.'

'I did this to myself,' Baradir repeated. 'Long ago. It's only a delayed result.' He looked for a moment at the three of them, clustered together, enraged at his fate and desperate to help. What had he done to deserve such love — least of all from them?

Why, nothing.

But perhaps, that might be changed. And if all that was left to him was magic and destruction...

'Look after each other,' he said.

'Father,' said Hanizani, and leapt forward. 'What are you—'

He did not hear the rest of her sentence, for he'd fallen through the floor.

No. He had fallen *into* the floor, and become part of it. How simple the process, in the end; he'd only had to wish, and in the blink of an eye there he was, merged and blended, as securely a part of his ill-fated palace as though he'd built himself into its walls all along.

He saw... everything. Fasani and Talandani and Hanizani still near. Yasmine and Ru and Sharan, elsewhere. Flickers of warmth and life and chaos all over the sprawling rooms of his many-storeyed form: guests, visitors, hostages trapped by Izebadd, living their straitened lives as best they could without their liberty.

And he saw, or sensed, Izebadd himself. The jinn-king crouched over his tiny, stolen kingdom like a great spider, glorying over the flies caught in his glittering web, devouring them piece by piece by piece.

'It's time, Izebadd,' he said.

Distantly, he was answered with a roar.

Izebadd

On came the broken old sorcerer, and Izebadd was ready for him. Flushed with the success of his gambit, he waited, laughing to himself. And that collection of vanquished limbs, that mess of polished, sorcerous organs gathered up its pitiful self and limped, a shattered mess, after the glory that was Izeb—

—*crash.* Thoughts abandoned Izebadd; pain blossomed instead, pain in every limbless part of him. His head filled up with the sharp *crack* of shattering glass, and he felt every splinter, as though he were a great window breaking into pieces. He cowered, shuddering, shock rendering him momentarily powerless.

How had the withered old sorcerer moved so fast, or hit so hard? He would swear Ibn Samar never did so before, not even when he had been a young man of living flesh, and at the heights of his power.

He was everywhere. Izebadd writhed like a snake, darted like a fox, rended and bit like all the wolves of the world together; to no avail. Wherever he turned, there was the shade of Ibn Samar, ablaze with power and wrath, and relentless. Izebadd twisted away; Ibn Samar caught him, and hauled him back. Izebadd attacked; buried his enemy in dirt, blew him apart, burned him in the fiercest fire, and still he came on, brushing every effort aside as though it were naught but a light breeze.

Izebadd broke and ran; Ibn Samar chased him down.

'How is this?' roared Izebadd, trapped. Were the walls getting nearer? They were. Inexorably, with taunting slowness, his world was shrinking.

'Did you think you had bested me?' growled Ibn Samar, only a voice, now, but too close. 'Fool,' he said with withering contempt. 'You've taken the mortal man out of me — what was left of him. And what remains? I am an elemental force, Majesty; magic only, and nothing else. And this,' he added with a snarl, 'is *my palace.*'

Something else caught Izebadd's attention, even as he shrank to the size of a pebble, the walls of his prison bearing down upon him with agonising pressure. A loosening, a dissolving; echoing spaces where strength had so lately been.

The palace, *his* palace, was falling down.

'You had better make up your mind, Father,' he heard his daughter say, soft as the dawn, inexorable as ice. She walked somewhere above, his grandchild by her side, and everything they touched turned to sand and fell away. 'You shall be freed, you perceive. My son commands it. And so shall everyone else in this abominable place.'

Had he not been bound and helpless, away he would have gone, and rebuilt the walls and windows his own family destroyed; raised up the minarets again, stronger than before. He would repel this ill-natured attack, eject his daughter and his grandchild (he'd make camels of them, like Ibn Samar's children; how they would enjoy that!), and whisk his precious palace far away.

But he could not. Rage though he might, exert himself as he would, Ibn Samar kept him bound and small and helpless. 'We will stay here,' said his tormentor, 'until your excellent descendants have finished their work. I congratulate you, by the by,' he added conversationally. 'Two such sorcerers in your family is a great compliment to you. They have more than enough power between them to reduce every inch of this place to dust.'

'And you permit it?' gasped Izebadd. 'Is this not *your* palace?'

'It is,' said Ibn Samar, icily cold. 'And its time is over.'

It took time, to unmake so large and magnificent a palace. At length, though, nothing remained of its glorious halls save a spill of sand in the desert, heaped piles of coloured dust shining oddly under the stars. Away went his guests, fleeing into the night in a great knot of jubilation.

Izebadd could only watch them go.

'Here,' said his grandchild, and set a vase down in the sand before Ibn Samar. The sorcerer had taken shape again, made of himself some human-like figure with arms and legs and every required thing. But he was as mortal as the water-fairy, whose touch still gleamed, cold and pale, upon his eye. As mortal, and as powerful.

To his secret shame, Izebadd quailed before the changes that his own anger had wrought. How had he not seen what the sorcerer would become?

He had not time to consider, for the world upended itself. Izebadd, sailing helplessly through the air, received a spinning, upside-down vision of his assembled foes: his daughter and his grandchild, sorrowful but resolute; the sorcerer of Xingqing, gravely expressionless; the woman Sharan, her turban larger than ever, exulting; the three offspring of Ibn Samar, all youthful anger (they had been better as camels, he thought, rebellious).

The last face he saw as he fell into the vase was Ibn Samar's polished visage and eerie, arcane glow. There was no exultation there, nor sorrow either. There was... nothing.

It was cold, at the bottom of the vase. When he looked up, he saw distant stars in a darkened sky — and then the face of his grandchild, peeping in.

'I did say I would get you out,' observed Riad.

'I am a prisoner still,' said Izebadd. 'Will you not vanquish this fool, and set me free?'

Riad appeared to consider the question; he even cast a sideways glance at, most probably, his mother.

'No,' he said. 'I don't think so.'

Yasmine's face appeared over the rim of the vase. 'You've become quite tiresome, Father,' she said. 'We'd like to release you, but you would only make a mess. Is that not so?'

'A mess?' spluttered Izebadd. 'A *mess*? I would make a kingdom, girl! I would make wonders this world has never seen! I would make magic, and light, and beauty, and *power*, and all the world would sit at my feet in awe! Ibn Samar is nothing to what I will do!' He went on, detailing his vision, his plans; and only some minutes later did he realise that the faces at the mouth of his prison were gone. His words bounced off the cool walls of the vase, echoing and forlorn, and there was only himself to hear them.

Fasani

Shivering under the cold, thin light of a few distant stars, Fasani made to wrap her robe more tightly about herself, and discovered it to be insufficient to the purpose. Instead, she inched nearer to her sisters, and the three huddled together, sharing what scant warmth they possessed. Inside the palace's smooth, glossy walls, the conditions beyond had been immaterial, for within all was comfort.

'F-father,' she said, her teeth chattering. 'When I said we'd lost all your things, I meant... the Twelvefold Pavilion, too.'

'Which was a shame,' agreed Hanizani. 'It would be the perfect thing to have, now that we are homeless again.'

'Not that it was wrong to take down the palace,' Fasani put in hastily, eyeing Yasmine and Riad as she spoke. They were holding some conversation of their own, and did not appear to hear her. 'That was well done.'

'It's better that it's gone,' said Talandani. 'But, it is also very cold out here.'

'Frightfully,' said Baradir, not altogether in his own voice, anymore. The word held a faint echo, as though it were spoken from some other plane of existence. Fasani tried not to look too long at him, for every familiar feature was gone. He was not human, not jinn; something profoundly magical, and because of that, a little frightening.

Warmth enfolded her, as though she wore a blanket over her shoulders. 'Is that better?' said Baradir.

'Yes. Thank you.' Fasani sneaked a look at him, and gaped, for the alien look of him was gone again, and his own face was back: the thick, black, grey-threaded hair and beard, the dark eyes, the prominent nose and strong jaw. He was smiling.

'Is that better?' he said again.

'Is it real?' said Hanizani.

'Only an illusion.'

'It's a good one,' Fasani decided.

Baradir acknowledged her approval with a brief touch to her hair, but he had patently abandoned the subject, and was looking around, as though he expected to see some solution to their predicament lying about in the sand. Fasani had no notion where their fellow palace-guests had gone, but that they meant to escape the punishing desert before dawn brought the heat and the sun, was evident enough, and no bad plan. 'Perhaps we ought to...' she said, trailing off, and pointing vaguely in the direction everyone else had gone in.

Yasmine, her debate with her son finished, said: 'We have sent them to the nearest town, Fasani, but *we* shall go to my tower, for the present.'

'Or mine,' put in Riad, with a smile Fasani did not like, for it was full of mischief.

'We would none of us last five minutes if we did that,' said Yasmine, and Riad's grin widened.

'Thank you,' said Baradir. 'But it's my hope neither will be necessary.'

'Oh?' said Yasmine, and looked about at the featureless expanse of sand and rock around them, much of it lost in the shadows of deep night.

'I have some promises yet to keep,' Baradir said, inclining his head in Ru's direction as he spoke. 'It is inconvenient, being without the pavilion — not that I am blaming you for its loss, girls, don't think that for an instant. And I had promised Ru the secrets of the palace's construction.'

Ru bowed. 'I am still curious,' he admitted.

'More than ever, I should think?' said Baradir, with a grin like Riad's, and Ru's answering smile was impish as well.

'There are possibilities,' he agreed.

'Might the two arts be combined, do you think?' said Baradir.

'Perhaps they might. With... some assistance.'

'Here we have two of the mighty jinn,' said Baradir, with a nod to Yasmine and Riad. 'Your arts and mine; three bright young women, full of ideas; and—' He smiled at Sharan, who stood silent and a little apart '—if we may borrow some little part of your powers, as well? In particular, your ways with the silks intrigue me...'

Sharan expressed herself willing, with an alacrity that resembled... relief? Fasani, surprised to see her linger, rather than dispatched to a nearby town with the others, wondered if perhaps she had unfinished business to transact.

Noticing the scrutiny, Sharan winked at Fasani, even as she unwound the great turban that held back her hair. There seemed more of it than ever, now, and it rippled out in a myriad of colours, reflecting starlight from its smooth-woven surface, and sending puffs of sand and palace-dust spiralling into the air.

When the silk came to rest, it lay in two separate pools. Sharan retrieved one, and rewound her turban, which looked in no way diminished by the loss of half of its fabric. The other she indicated with a graceful gesture of one thin hand, and said: 'It is yours.'

Baradir positively beamed, and made her a courtly bow. 'Now we shall spin wonders,' he promised, and as he spoke all the eerily-shining sand that had once been his palace of marvels rose up, and began, as he had said, to spin.

'You're making a new palace,' said Hanizani, retreating from the mess of sand and dust that rose, higher and higher, towards the stars.

'A better one?' said Talandani, following.

'A better one,' agreed Baradir. 'More comfortable, for one.'

'More portable,' said Ru, at work with Sharan's silk. In his hands it folded up, flew out again, billowed and tossed, and Fasani watched in fascination.

'More benign?' said Yasmine, with a lift of her aristocratic brow.

'Much more,' said Baradir.

Riad, intent upon Baradir's workings, stretched out a hand. Fasani could not sense what he had done, but that there came some change to the way the sand twisted and spun was clear enough, and it began to sparkle in a thousand colours.

'That's clever,' said Baradir, and flashed the boy a smile. 'Thank you.'

Riad, in fact, looked like a boy at last, for his wolf's head and other animal parts were no longer in evidence. He was a few years older than Hanizani and Talandani, Fasani now thought, and well-looking, his tumbled hair the colour of his mother's, his face open and full of humour (even if it was the wicked kind). His own smile blossomed under Baradir's praise, in naïve gratification. *What a brother he'd make*, Fasani thought, and decided at once to arrange it.

Yasmine joined her son, and she and Riad and Baradir manipulated the glorious sand with arts Fasani could not feel, but with a palpable skill. Ru and Sharan, working together, caused the silks of her turban to spread in a wide, fluid expanse over the ground, where it waited, a cloth floor needing only walls and a ceiling to make of it a dwelling.

'Well, then, how shall it look?' Baradir called, and he was looking at Fasani, Hanizani and Talandani. 'What shall we have in our new home?'

The three exchanged glances.

'It could look like your house in Sulanah,' said Hanizani. 'Only, not ruined.'

'With a garden behind, please,' said Talandani.

'Can I have my room back?' said Fasani. 'With the pictures in the walls?'

'My house in Sulanah?' Baradir, thunderstruck, gazed at Yasmine.

'We went there,' she said. 'It is how we found you. The palace held some link, perhaps unconsciously made.'

Baradir blinked. 'And that's what you want?' he said to Fasani, and her sisters. 'No palace? Just a house?'

'You did say comfortable,' Hanizani pointed out. 'The palace was never that.'

Fasani, unable to escape the conviction that her father was disappointed, said: 'Maybe it can be both?'

'How can it be both?' said Hanizani, with some scorn.

But Baradir was smiling. 'Of course it can be both. If a building may be made to rise out of a bundle of silk, and travel about the world, why, it can be anything else that we want.'

And then, there it was: the same modest dwelling in which Ibn Samar had so long ago been born, though it was shining and new, more handsome and more colourful than ever its predecessor had been. Verdure bloomed at every window, spilling down the walls, and soft lights shone within.

The front door — which, if one squinted and tilted one's head just *so,* resembled fluttering panels of silk — stood open.

Fasani ran inside, crowing with delight. The floor underfoot was all silk, and soft, like Baradir's tent; but everything else was glass, bright and clear and magical.

The moment she entered the modest ground-floor room, those colours shifted, and showed her that vision of the old palace she'd always loved: a vibrant presence in a dark, starlit night, glimmering with a promise it had never quite fulfilled.

'This next one will be better,' she assured it.

'Who are you talking to?' said Hanizani, coming in behind her.

Fasani pointed. 'The old palace.'

'I don't see a palace,' said Talandani. 'I see a garden.'

'It is neither,' said Hanizani. 'It's a city, like Sulanah.'

'It is whatever you want,' said Baradir, with Yasmine on his arm. 'And this is only the beginning. You'll see. There's much more to come.'

Ru prowled about the place, inspecting the scenes — what did he see, wondered Fasani? Whatever visions he saw, he chose not to share what they were, but went all around the room, smiling with quiet contentment. 'Do you think,' said he, when his circuit was complete, and addressing Baradir, 'that it would be possible to make more of these?'

'More Thousandfold Palaces? Perhaps it might.'

Ru's smile broadened, and with a happy sigh, he sat in a silk-clad chair which obligingly materialised behind him. 'They will be my greatest work,' he said simply.

'Mine, too,' Baradir agreed.

'Not mine,' said Riad, sprawling upon the floor in a corner. 'I intend to make something even greater, one day.'

'Like what?' Fasani demanded.

He waved this away, his eyes closing. 'I don't know yet. That's for later.'

Fasani looked for Sharan, but did not see her. Going to the door, she looked out, and saw the sorceress standing diffidently outside, gazing upon the silk-and-glass structure with an expression faintly wistful.

'But, Sharan,' said Fasani. 'Aren't you coming in?'

'May I?' said Sharan.

'It's your Thousandfold Palace, too,' said Fasani, and held open the door.

Sharan, with a low bow, permitted herself to be ushered inside.

The silken doors closed upon Fasani and her mismatched family: Baradir, once a sorcerer, now something new; Yasmine and Riad (and Izebadd), the jinn; Ru of the Xingqing and Sharan of the maps; and her sisters of heart and blood, never far from her. They closed upon a starlit desert, where once Ibn Samar's palace had stood.

In the morning, when the sun rose and day dawned and Fasani's family awoke, Riad was the first to go to the door, and open it.

'Ha!' he said, in delight. 'We're somewhere else.'

Fasani, scrambling after, beheld tall trees with red-tinted leaves, and a ground carpeted in white. A wide road wound between the graceful boughs, and vanished into the distance, beckoning.

The sun shone, high above; but so, peculiarly, did the moon.

'I have no knowledge of this place,' said Baradir, coming up behind.

'Nor I,' said Yasmine.

'Shall we go and look?' said Fasani, itching to step outside, and into that odd whiteness. Cold radiated off it; she felt it even from inside the door.

'Always,' said Sharan, the silks of her turban in her hands. She stepped out, and threw the fabric far. Inks inscribed themselves upon the surface, a dozen maps appearing.

'Ah,' she said. 'We are in the forests of Tanpoba.' Winding up her turban once more, she set off down the road, calling over her shoulder, 'Are you coming?'

Fasani, ablaze with excitement, looked to Baradir, who smiled down upon her.

'Unquestionably,' he said. 'Let's go.'

Also By Charlotte E. English

The Wonder Tales:
Faerie Fruit
Gloaming
Sands and Starlight
Summertide
Ravensby Od

Tales of Aylfenhame:
Miss Landon and Aubranael
Miss Ellerby and the Ferryman
Bessie Bell and the Goblin King
Mr. Drake and My Lady Silver

www.charlotteenglish.com